SHADOWPLAY:
A TALE

BY NORMAN LOCK

ellipsis
· · ·
press

ISBN 0-9637536-3-0

ISBN-13 978-0-9637536-3-2

Cover photograph and book design by Eugene Lim

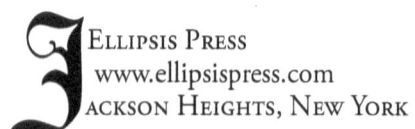

ELLIPSIS PRESS
www.ellipsispress.com
JACKSON HEIGHTS, NEW YORK

Also by Norman Lock

FICTION:
A History of the Imagination
Trio: Grim Tales, Joseph Cornell's Operas, and Émigrés
Notes to 'The Book of Supplemental Diagrams for
    Marco Knauff's Universe'
Land of the Snow Men
The Long Rowing Unto Morning
The King of Sweden

DRAMA:
Water Music
Favorite Sports of the Martyrs
The House of Correction
The Contract
Mounting Panic
The Sinking Houses
Women in Hiding
The Shining Man (published in *Two Plays for Radio)*
The Primate House
Money, Power & Greed
The Book of Stains

POETRY:
Cirque du Calder

FILM:
The Body Shop

To Marco Knauff, Eugene Lim, Kathryn Rantala,
Cooper Renner, and Derek White.

And for my wife, Helen, with love and gratitude.

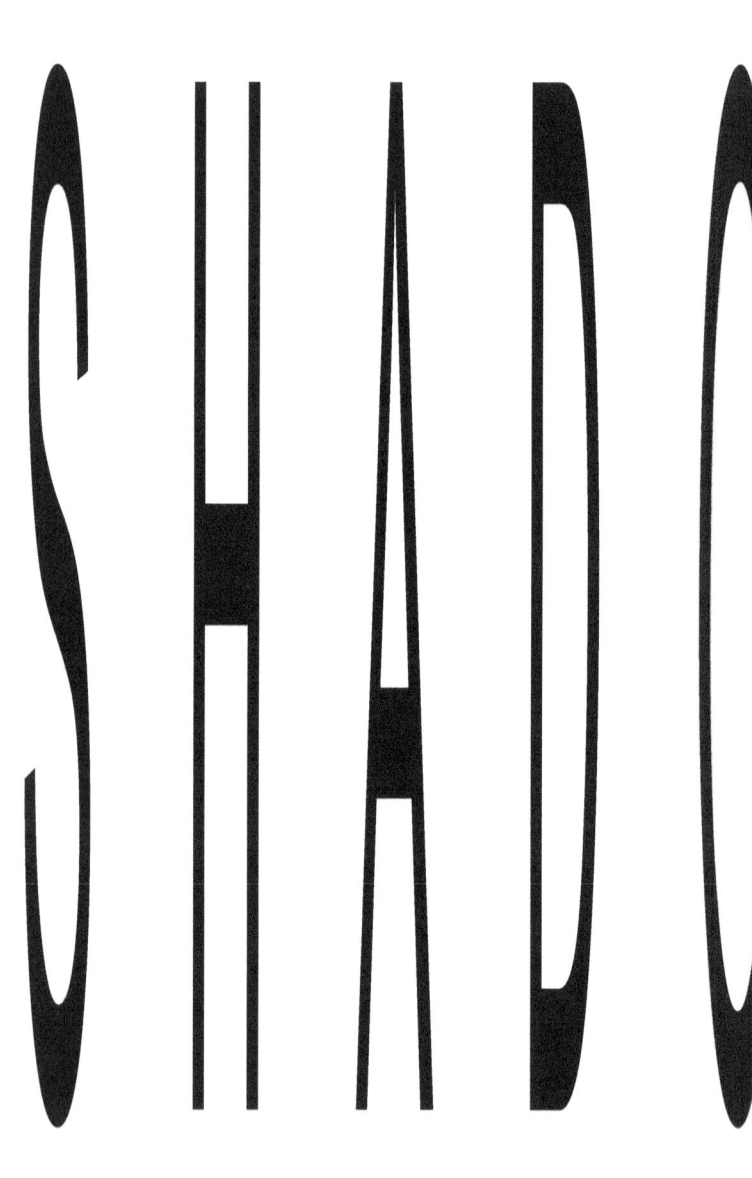

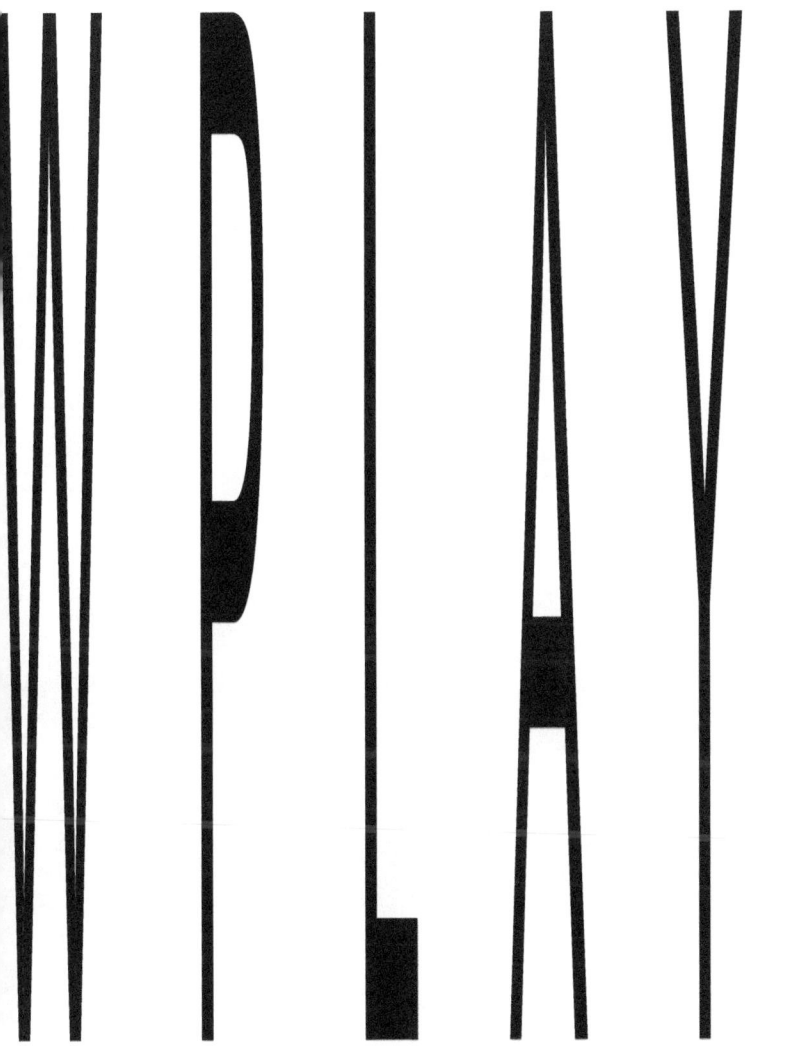

PLAY

BY NORMAN LOCK

Be silent, then, for danger is in words.
  —Christopher Marlowe, *Doctor Faustus*

In Java during the reign of King Senapati, a master of the shadow-puppet theater heard, by chance from a Portuguese sailor, the story of Orpheus and Eurydice.

PART ONE

Guntur was already past fifty when he was granted, by virtue of a supreme artistry or a special destiny, the power to possess the woman he adored since he had first seen her standing shyly in his puppet theater. He had been forty then, his hair not yet gray or his back bent. Candra had come from the *batik* clothmaker to buy puppets, and for six afternoons Guntur had questioned her from behind the story-screen about her life. During the sixth night, she was taken by a fever whose origin might have been Guntur's own ardent interest in her, his desire to ravish her of words. For ten years after that first death, he sought her among the shadows while the theater remained closed, the puppets shut away. At the end of the tenth year, Guntur took up the puppets again and with one of them, Arjuna, brought Candra back from the dead. Had he refused the gift and resisted the arrogance its acceptance entailed, the artistry and destiny (which for a time exalted him) would not have exacted so absolute a punishment.

Candra was unhappy to live always inside the shadow theater, which itself seemed composed of shadows. They clung like soot from the oil lamp to the edges of the table and the strings of the *rebab*. They collected like rain in the hollows worn into the floor. Shadows obscured the faces of the musicians when they turned toward the darkness as if seeing there Sinta abducted by Rahwana, the Monster King, whose story Guntur performed behind the illuminated screen. Were Candra to leave the theater and its enchantment, she would return to the sleep from which Guntur and Arjuna had wakened her. This, she knew when she did leave, finally, to follow her lover there. She stepped outside and, in an instant, died.

1.

Guntur is once again undone by grief. He weeps but is not inconsolable, for he knows how Candra can be restored to him—knows by what secret ways she can be brought back. (That she could have chosen death is a possibility he rejects.) He asks two Sikhs, who are watching him kneel beside a woman in the street, to carry her body into the theater.

Guntur has only to make the puppet rods dance at the door to the Land of the Dead to draw the woman out of its iron embrace. He has only to take in his hands the buffalo-horn rods to send the

Warrior Prince, Arjuna, on his difficult way across death's doorway to release, for a second time, Candra from her dream of life. Although Arjuna's journey to Yama's island kingdom will be painful for Guntur while he sits bent over his puppets behind the story-screen, with the music of the *gamelan* and the *rebab* heard only in his mind now that the musicians are home sleeping—he would suffer this and more to have Candra with him again.

It is after all a small thing for a *dalang*, who long ago mastered his shadow art, to work the puppet rods and, with them, walk into Death on the legs of his puppet warrior. It would be the puppet master who enters the lovers' pavilion. It would be he who lifts the sleeping woman from the soldier's arms and carries her across the threshold of the afterworld, through the nothingness that separates it from the village with its huts and pigs and squabbles and dust, into the theater where Guntur has performed ever since he was a young man. It will be Guntur in the form of Arjuna, who rescues Candra.

The sleeping woman whose hands are blue.

His heart wishes it. His mind does, and his body— his hands, which for forty years have manipulated the goat-skin puppets behind the diaphanous white screen. His hands move as if they are themselves *wayang*, as if they are no longer part of himself but belong, instead, to them. His hands move with no more thought given them than to the spoon with which he eats his rice and fish. They move with no more thought than a Dutch soldier's wife gives to the needles as she knits out of a strand of yarn, woolen hose for her husband, which he will not wear in the intense Java heat; but knit she must—obedient to the will of her hands and, perhaps, also of the wool. So, too, a *dalang* knits out of shadows the Hindu stories his people love, not knowing whether his hands will it or the stories themselves do.

Guntur's hands have wandered the ancient realms of the *Ramayana* and *Mahabharata*—have made formidable journeys during a thousand nights while the oil lamp casts his puppets' shadows onto the story-screen. The flat parchment puppets—*wayang kulit*—and the hands of their master are one. This is true of all *dalangs*. Unlike them, however, Guntur once went to the Land of the Dead. He became Arjuna and brought Candra back with him to the shadow theater. (Unless it was that Arjuna became Guntur; it is impossible to say in whose mind the story was written.)

Now, Guntur's mind and hands are bent on one thing: to deliver Candra from death and, though death be a paradise, to return with her to Surakarta.

Why, then, does he hesitate to light the oil lamp and take from the banana-tree trunk in which it rests the goat-skin puppet; to play in his mind the two-stringed instrument, whose songs are as intricate and seductive as the sea's; to hold the puppet rods and send Arjuna where Candra, whose hands are dyed indigo, is dreaming? Why does Guntur not hurry with Arjuna to where there is neither time nor words nor dust?

2.

"You mustn't!" the old woman admonishes Guntur, taking from him the puppet Arjuna, so that the *dalang* cannot travel a second time beyond death's door and return with Candra. Here, there is only a likeness of death. In the room's heavy shadows and in the single shadow that is night, death admires its image as if in a mirror. When the rain beats mournfully against the leaves and the thatched roof, it is as if the night sea were hurrying into the room's corners and the spaces between its rafters.

"You mustn't!" she repeats, roughly handling the puppet as though she intends to cripple Arjuna.

Guntur stares at her as he would a ghost who has entered his room from a seam in the air. He sees Arjuna gripped in her hand and wonders, idly, if the pressure of her fingers hurts the Pandava warrior, whose invisible presence the puppet signifies. For a moment he forgets Candra—forgets his determination to abduct her from the blue pavilion where she sleeps in the arms of the dead soldier, enfolded together as if death were a silk shroud wound about them both.

For a moment, Guntur does not see Candra where

she is sleeping without end—does not see her asleep as though in a mist, a shimmering heat, or the waning light. Now it is this old woman he sees, who seems to have arrived from the passageway connecting life and its reflection—so suddenly did she appear. He grasps her wrist to prevent her flight from the shadow theater with his puppet. But she has no intention of leaving.

The woman may be herself a ghost quickened by the *dalang*'s hand on her wrist while in her hand Arjuna has halted in his preparations for the difficult journey. There are many such formidable women in Hindu stories. May not this woman be one of them? Might she not have left the shadow world, attracted by the lamp light wavering on the cotton screen? The theater is silent beneath the black trees; what music there is, plays only in Guntur's mind. Perhaps this fierce woman has possessed the puppet master's hand clenching her wrist. Perhaps she has cast her shadow, from where the *Ramayana* and the *Mahabharata* are eternally occurring, into the theater— drawn by a light and music unheard by all save the two of them.

"You must not wake her!"

She releases her grip on the puppet, but in her eyes Guntur sees that she has not relented. He inserts the puppet rod in the banana-tree trunk, letting Arjuna rest. Lying between Guntur and the story screen, the trunk has the heft of a man's arm.

"Who are you?" he asks.

"Candra's aunt."

And Guntur remembers how, after Candra's mysterious first death, he had gone to beg of her aunt the young woman's wooden bangles.

"I did not recognize you," he says, letting go her arm.

"You destroyed her once—now let her be!" The weak light seems to shrink from the woman's fury as though her gusting anger shook the flame in the unchimneyed lamp, which yielded its small and timid fire to the room's expectant darkness. She may be only a mortal woman; but in her rage against Guntur and his indecency, she is like Amba, an exemplar of supernatural vengeance. Guntur feels the storm of her buffeting him, and his hands tremble so that he cannot take up Arjuna and with him drive the woman from the playhouse.

Arjuna rests, his puppet rod in the hollow green trunk. He is without resolve, emptied of purpose—now that Guntur's will, like a boat submissive to a powerful tide, has ebbed away from the seaward journey.

3.

If Guntur was destined to live among shadows, Candra was fashioned for bright sun. She was born in the light and twice died when darkness was already gathering in the corners of the room where she lay waiting to be engulfed by night.

Her father was a fisherman. Her mother tended fields of sweet potatoes and rice. Their house was raised on stilts above the marsh grass. The house looked out upon the Java Sea, into which Candra's father disappeared each morning, early, when the sun trembled on the horizon, and from which each night he appeared out of the darkening sky when the fishing was done.

Like a *wayang*. Ghost.

There were the three of them together; and then a fourth, Lastri, was born.

As the sisters grew, they became bound in affection—each to each and each one also to the mother or father. Lastri followed her mother into the fields while Candra was already in the boat when the sun came up over the rim of the world, making light spill across the sand, turning it pink, then gold, then white. The sand would be white until the sun's leaving turned the grains to rubies, which shone until the light was put out suddenly in the sky and the shadows that all the while had been lengthening joined to become night.

Her father was almost always silent. He spoke only of what was important to know in a boat far from land.

"You must coil the rope this way," he said, showing Candra how to make the rope lie flat on the bottom of the boat. "In the water, it will come alive again, like an eel."

"You must hold the net this way," he said, showing Candra how to gather the corners of the net in both hands. "So that when it is thrown, it will turn in the air like a wheel before falling into the water."

"You must reef the sail this way," the father said,

showing the girl how to fold and tie the sail. "So that the increasing wind will not overwhelm the boat."

In the boat, he spoke little, preferring to listen to what the wind and water sang. When he spoke, he did so with deliberation so that Candra would understand the importance of what he said. The only exception to his solemnity, which she, too, observed, was the nonsense words they sang to encourage the fish to swim into the net.

The nights were dark but not entirely when the weather was fine, for the vast quantity of stars was like a shining dust against the blackness. So many stars were there that they seemed to sift down onto the sea and, when the tide was high, into the tiny bays that coiled among the marsh grasses. The stars seemed also to cling to the tops of the palm leaves—their bottoms blacker than night itself.

Later, inside the house, Candra would sit mending a torn net under the oil lamp, or eating fish and rice sweetened with coconut, or singing with her father the nonsense song they sang, waiting for the fish. Lastri helped her mother to wash and put away the pots. Such a division as this is natural when the work must be divided. This story is not about the envy of sisters or the jealousy of parents. This story tells of an impossible love, which overrules reason and the boundary the gods have ordained between life and death.

4.

Candra was fifteen when she met a boy who, like her, went each day to fish almost to the sun's doorway into morning. The boy had moved with his family from another place on the sea coast. That place was so much like this as to be almost the same—was, in fact, identical except for its name. Many times it is only the names of things that make a difference to anyone—that is to say: words.

Candra's father did not like the boy, because the name of the boy's family had never been heard before in the village. When he saw him with his daughter one afternoon during the rains when fishing was not possible, his heart raged, though the distance that separated Candra and the boy was such that they had to throw their words into the rain and wind to be heard. When a word was lost in the clamor, they laughed, thinking this a marvelous prank played on them by the storm.

Candra's father strode through the rain like a crane that, with its beak, spears small silver fish in the flooded marsh. He strode on legs stiff as those of the *wayang kulit*, which he had never seen, because there was no *dalang* in his village. He went to the boy and struck him.

"She is not for you!" he shouted so that not a single word was torn away by the wind on its way to their ears.

Candra had not thought of the boy as her lover.

Love had yet to enter her heart and put there its roses and its thorns.

They stood on the beach wet with rain, which had turned the white sand black. The sea could not be heard, except in the uncanny silence when the wind flagged. The sea was gray, like the rain, with here and there white creases made by the wind. They stood, looking at each other: the father at the boy, the boy at him, and Candra at the two of them together. The father wiped his eyes of rain and, turning, strode back along the black beach the way he had come. His shoulders stooped in weariness and grief, he did not turn to look at his daughter, though he wished it. Because he did not turn to see her standing in perplexity, he would not be able to remember her face after she had left him. This was his punishment.

But this is not the story of two lovers parted by their families. Although sad stories are told of it—this is not one of them. This story concerns Guntur's love for Candra, which she did not return.

After the rain, the black sand crusted and turned gray. Its surface was pitted by the rain and by sand crabs. It would turn white again in the sun; but the crust would remain, like stale bread, until it broke underfoot. It would not be Candra, who broke the stiff sand.

5.

Before the rains had stopped, Candra was sent to live with her mother's sister. To live far from the sea and a sun that seemed to rise like a great fish from out the red water of morning—this, for her, was banishment. She missed how the boat jumped suddenly over the waves when the morning wind made the sail fat. The boat hurried toward the sun, pulling itself out of the sea, while night slipped backwards across the violet sky, leaving behind only shadows of itself. The shadows lay down on the sea, turning the backs of the waves black; and on the land, they sprawled across the fields like men who have drunk too much palm wine.

At night, returning with hampers heavy with red anchovies dreaming on a bed of seaweed, Candra had watched for the lights of the village, trembling in the mist rolling across the water. The water around the boat was blacker than the night, and the forest visible on the other side of the mist was blacker still. The sea had lapped the sides of the boat, and the sharp keel had cut deep into the water because of the weight of the catch, and everywhere were the mysteries of darkness.

Hers was a banishment she did not understand, for nowhere had she made a place for the boy—not in her heart or in her thoughts when they were apart. She had not once dreamed of him. She dreamed often of the sea sweeping over the beach—its jade edge chipped and breaking on the uneven sand. She

12

dreamed, too, of the boat. She saw the yellow hemp ropes coiled on the bottom and the sail, which her father carried home at night. Sometimes she dreamt of her mother and sister kneeling in the sweet potato field or standing in the sky reflected in a rice field's black water. But not often, for seldom had she gone to the fields. Her place had been in the boat.

"What is that sweetness in the air?" she would say to her father as the slack sail suddenly caught the wind.

She had asked each morning this same question when she felt the wind stir. Her father had answered always the same: "It is the wind blowing through the cinnamon groves."

"So far?"

Now each day Candra went with her aunt to make dye, while her sister, Lastri, took her place in the boat that waited for the wind to fatten its sail so that it might fly toward the new sun and return with hampers heavy with anchovies.

The anchovies were red. The sun was red at first light and also at evening before the night closed like a lid on a hinge whose creaking was the sound of birds leaving the sea. In the dying sun, red and violet rags of light were spread across the sky.

Love had yet to lay its roses and thorns at the door of Candra's heart, which was as a room waiting to be entered.

Candra made indigo dye, and soon her hands

became stained like her aunt's. She stood at a vat and mixed indigo leaves with molasses sugar and lime, and never did she think of the boy except as someone with whom to walk by the sea, to hunt among its broken crockery for nautilus and amphora shells, and to make stories about people on the sea bottom or on an island beyond the sun. She mixed indigo leaves, molasses sugar, and lime, then added sap from the *tinggi* tree. The dye was used to make *batik* cloth prized by the rich. She thought of the boy rarely and did not regret that she would never see him again.

For Candra, *mbatik manah* had yet to happen. *Mbatik manah*, which means: "to have drawn upon the heart," as cloth receives its *batik* pattern. The boy had been no more than sand, which the sea—in its changes—uncovered only to cover again. Love, for Candra, was what arrived from the earth's four corners, bringing integers of an incalculable sum, as pebbles are brought by pilgrims to leave on holy ground. She had not yet renounced the love of diverse things in favor of one man destined to write his name upon her heart.

She was in love with the *melati* blossoms and with the wind bearing odors of nutmeg, of cinnamon, and of the river—and with the river itself, which played music among the reeds and the shallow's white and yellow stones. She was in love with the dusty yard where chickens muttered querulously while they printed in the dust their curious signs, which she could read no more than she could those carved onto the temple walls. And the slant of sun when it rose each morning behind the cinnamon grove and the moon—how it trembled in puddles after rain. These, she loved, together with the plain brown cloth her aunt fashioned into sarongs, the wood bowls on the table where she saw evidence of time as it had unfolded for this, her new family: knife scar and pot scorch and the smooth places where her uncle's sinewy forearms rested.

She loved the days when heaven's radiant beings came down as though on ladders to put out time's lidless eye in a blaze of effulgence. Then, would Candra walk to the temple with her friend Liat— both adorned with flowers and shells brought from the sea by a trader to sell in the marketplace. It is not known what words they said to one another, but they must have spoken as young girls speak—of bangles and silk cloth; and if they spoke of young men, it was only with the vague desire to sit across the table with someone whose forearms rested on the smooth wood or to stand together in the yard and watch the sudden darkness fall.

Candra was not without flaw. (Only in the story Guntur told himself during the long absence of her first death was she exemplary; he had seen her briefly and imperfectly, after all, through his theater's story-screen.) Like many other girls, she was sullen at times and at times covetous of the fine sarongs and gold bangles worn by wealthy girls who passed on their way to weddings, in the flowery carts driven by Sikhs. She was capable of spite and more than once had lied to her aunt—admittedly about small things.

By this, I would have you understand that Candra was in no way extraordinary. She made indigo dye, with blue hands like those of all the other women who stood with her at the vats. She listened to their stories and sang for them sometimes the nonsense song she and her father used to sing as they had waited for the fish to wake. She wondered if Lastri sang it now or was all silent in the boat except for the noise of the rope against the side as they dragged up the net.

When Candra dreamed of the sea as she did often, she heard always a music she could neither recognize nor remember—drowned in the noises of the street at the instant of waking.

6.

One day, the man who oversaw the copying of *batik* patterns onto cloth sent Candra to the *dalang* to see whether he had puppets to sell. Tiny holes pierced in the puppet's painted surface added detail and interest to the figure. By blowing powdered charcoal through them, a pattern could be laid on the cloth as if by a stencil. *Wayang* patterns were favored by courtiers because of their complexity, and the clothmakers eagerly bought puppets that a *dalang* no longer considered worthy of his theater—those whose leather was worn or which no longer danced jauntily at the ends of their puppet rods.

Although she had seen *wayang* at the *batik* clothmaker's, Candra had never before been in a shadow theater. Outside, four *gamelan* musicians were resting in the shade of a pavilion. The flute player was idly waving with his flute at a persistent fly. A *saron* and a *kempul* player shared a dish of cold cucumber and noodles. One of the *kendhang* players lay with his feet in the sun.

"Please, I want to see the *dalang*," Candra said, smiling from out of the sun at the man whose bare feet were like two birds bathing in the dust.

"He's inside," he answered, not bothering to look at her.

"He's playing with his puppets," said the flute player, who ceased a moment his fitful persecution of the fly.

The two eating cold cucumber and noodles said nothing.

Candra left her shoes in the doorway.

Stepping inside the theater, she heard the thin music of the two-stringed *rebab*. She heard a voice rising and falling behind a white screen, reciting the story of Sinta's ravishing and her rescue by the Monkey King. She heard the puppet rods clicking. She saw *wayang*—their puppet shadows moving behind the story screen. The voice rose and fell inside the room where the thin light falling through small, high windows did nothing to lessen the shadows.

Like a song, she thought, such as the sea makes when the boat is hurrying over the waves—the wind fat in the sail and the taut lines whining.

She stood without moving until Guntur, the *rebab*, and the puppet rods fell silent and the *wayang* were still. In the silence that grew in the dusky space, she lifted an arm to make a wooden bangle clack against another. Guntur stepped from behind the screen—Rahwana, the Monster King, in his hands.

His eyes asked her what she wanted. She saw the question in them and also shyness.

"Do you have any puppets to sell?" she asked. "For *batik* patterns?"

"Come tomorrow!" he snarled so that she stepped back and the two bangles sounded again on her arm. She lowered her face at once and, with her eyes on the floor, did not see his.

He turned abruptly and went behind the white cotton screen. Had she looked up, she would have seen his own shadow there.

The light in the room was like dusk that sifts through the trees as the birds return to rest there, or like the fragrant dust powdering the hands of the cinnamon-maker.

One bangle had fallen against another when she had let her arm fall in dismay.

She had not seen the puppet master's eyes.

7.

Before Guntur uttered his first word, his father had made a place for him in his workshop. He played with scraps of parchment, which his father shaped into puppets and later pierced with a needle to outline the patterns his craftsmen would paint with exquisite skill. Guntur's mother had died a short time after he was born. His father had grieved and performed the rites prescribed for him, and then returned to his workshop—there to resume his painstaking craft.

His puppets were admired for their workmanship, purity of color, and the ease with which the rods could be manipulated by a puppet master. They moved with a precision and grace surpassing the work of many other excellent makers of shadow puppets.

His father watched with satisfaction as Guntur one day picked up a small chisel with the wish to shape the leather into a puppet.

"You are not ready to cut into the leather," he told the boy severely, so that he would understand the importance of *wayang,* which means shadow or ghost. "If you want one day to make a shadow puppet, begin with this." He showed his young son how to smooth the chiseled leather by rolling it with a bottle. "Afterwards, the leather will be primed, smoothed once more with the bottle, and then painted. No step may be omitted, and none can be hurried."

The puppets made in his workshop were found

in shadow theaters as far away as Surakarta. *Dalangs* traveled many days to buy his puppets, as you might if you wished to own a piece of jade or a Persian miniature.

When Guntur was ten years old, he was allowed to cut into the leather with the smallest chisel, in recognition of the sureness of his hand and the intelligence with which he considered the figure's intricacy.

"Hold the chisel so," his father told him, demonstrating the technique which was, in his hands, effortless. "The unwanted leather must be removed with patience. No step may be omitted, and none can be hurried."

While he worked, Guntur thought about the meaning of *wayang*.

8.

Ten years passed since Guntur had taken chisel in hand and carved a puppet from a piece of buffalo leather. They passed quietly in that workshop where the concentration needed to carve, pierce, paint, and to prepare the joints and buffalo-horn rods discouraged all but the most important exchange of words; and those, most often, were between the master and his workers. Reticent by nature, Guntur found the monastic customs of the workshop agreeable. He liked the silence that was for him as an unheard music written by motes of dust moving lazily in the light falling from the windows. Like someone tired by a long journey, the light had not strength or will enough to cross the room and take possession of its shadows. Guntur did not speak to the master unless spoken to, though they were father and son; and the master, acknowledging his son's wish to be left alone, spoke less and less to him. Guntur applied himself to the *wayang*, savoring the smell of dust mixed with paint and the scent of pine, which arrived on the east wind, and, in its season, the rain.

He thought of each puppet as if it might by his industry become animate. He applied himself assiduously during the weeks of its creation—finishing it at last because he could spare it no more time but all the while believing that, were he able to devote another day, another hour, he could give it life. He did not confide in his father this thought, nor did he know if the master or any *dalang* thought it.

He liked the rainy season more than any other time because it shut him away from the world. The heavy rains intervened in the world, taking air's place just as fire did. To be shut away was, for Guntur, happiness.

To be shut away by water and also, perhaps, by fire.

At thirteen, his skill in making *wayang* was very nearly that of a master's.

"Will you become a master puppet-maker?" his father asked, watching with satisfaction as his son added purple to Gatotkaca's crown with a fine boar-bristle brush.

"No," the boy answered.

"What then?"

"A *dalang*."

Fire signifies ambition and also passionate devotion. They are the same and are joined in the image of fire; and by a fire is the ambitious man, the passionate man, consumed.

9.

One day, an illustrious *dalang* arrived from Surakarta. For many years, he had bought the puppets for his shadow theater from the workshop of Guntur's father. Each year an assistant had traveled east to Malang and returned with them, pressed between broad leaves, in a teak box. But this time, the puppet master himself came, wishing to see where the incomparable *wayang* were made. He arrived at the workshop in the evening, when the violet rags of sunset were already caught in the trees thronging the western hills. Guntur's father attended him, serving tea and rice-flour cakes to restore the old man, whom the journey had tired.

While the *dalang* took his refreshment and listened to the *wayang*-maker recite the history of his workshop, he became intent on a voice in another room, telling an unfamiliar story concerning Rama. So closely did he follow it that, soon, he no longer heard Guntur's father, though he nodded politely from time to time so as not to offend him. The voice rose and fell, its tone modulating between that reserved for the sublime and for the monstrous—occasionally becoming melodious to render the character of a princess. The story was fantastic—one not found in the *Ramayana*. In its musical aspects, the voice demonstrated a precocious refinement of technique in spite of its apparent youthfulness. When the story ended and the voice gave way to silence, the *dalang* looked at the puppet-maker, who had ceased speaking out of respect for his guest's struggle to satisfy ceremony and curiosity, both.

"My son," he said in answer to his guest's unspoken question. "He wishes to become a *dalang*."

"I should like to speak to him."

The puppet-maker bowed and led the *dalang* into the next room.

10.

"I have never heard before this story of Rama."

Guntur bowed toward the shadow master and said: "Not knowing well the stories in the *Ramayana* or the *Mahabharata*, I invent my own."

The shadow master rebuked him: "There are *dalangs* who embellish the stories; there are some, I know, who invent their own. But I frown on invention. It is presumptuous. *Dalangs* are custodians of a thousand-year-old tradition. It is for you to learn its forms."

The young man bowed again, murmuring that he was compelled to tell stories of his own.

"What compels you?"

Guntur, whose eyes were always elsewhere than on those who spoke to him, answered that he did not know, but that it seemed to be something inside him, which he could not quell. "An unrest."

"Unrest?" asked the *dalang*, who was not surprised—or if he was, his interrogative tone revealed nothing more than the wish for clarification.

"It is like a thorn," Guntur said earnestly, though his eyes remained on the floor between them. "Or a pebble that has gotten into my shoe, or a seed caught between my teeth, or…." He stopped saying what it was like, finding his similes unsatisfactory. "It is a feeling that something is in me that must be pulled out."

The *dalang* possessed the wisdom of all who have lived a long time with stories concerning the creation of the world. He was silent a while to allow the words that the young man had uttered—perhaps for the first time to himself—to find their way. Then he spoke: "It is as the makers of *batik* cloth say, '*Mbatik manah.*' Storytelling has written itself on your heart. If it is truly so, you must follow the patterns already drawn. Invention is a sacrilege, for the stories have already happened and are happening and will happen and cannot happen in any other way. They are like a map drawn long ago of a remote region. The land there is unchanging and so must the map be also."

Guntur bowed a third time. This time it was not only in observance of custom. The old man's words had entered his understanding.

The old *dalang* sat on the outside of the story-screen. He had not sat there since he had become a master of shadows fifty years before. Knowing the young man's shyness, he nodded for him to sit on the storyteller's side of the cotton screen. The old man's will was legible in his eyes and in his body's gestures, which were invitations impossible to refuse. Guntur sat and recited his history while the last of daylight spent itself traveling across the sea, which rose and fell far from Malang.

His father left the room to dismiss the workers and to shut up the workshop for the night.

Even when night had entered the room, Guntur did not stop to light the oil lamp, nor did he cease in the recitation of his history.

11.

Through the story-screen, Guntur told the old man how he had played with scraps of buffalo hide or goat's skin; how he had spent his boyhood in the workshop learning how to shape puppets from leather parchment, to pierce patterns onto them with a needle, to paint the patterns with bright colors. He told the old man—always speaking through the cotton screen even after the light had gone out of the room—of his wish to become a master of a shadow theater.

He did not tell him of his desire to be left alone and of his happiness when the rains came and shut him in with the noise of their drumming on the banana leaves and on the workshop roof. But these desires would not have surprised the *dalang*, who knew, from how the young man's eyes wandered away from his, of his shyness and reserve.

Guntur said:

"The boy, who lived in his father's workshop and became nearly as skillful as his father, grew to love puppets. He played with them as one would a doll, inventing stories—though it was a sacrilege—in which princes loved princesses, who were abducted by monsters and giants, and then rescued by their lovers with the help of Arjuna, his favorite."

The puppet master did not think it strange that Guntur should refer to himself as if he were another; the young man was a storyteller, and it was impolite to tell stories of oneself.

"The boy told stories of journeying to the Land of the Dead and imagined the long and difficult way there, on foot and by elephant. These and other adventures did the boy tell himself and—in their telling—went himself on them. Or at least his hands did."

Guntur said:

"His hands were becoming puppet characters, were becoming indistinguishable from them.

"'If my hands were Arjuna,' he thought, 'and if on a thousand nights they rode on an elephant toward the opening in the mountain that led to the Land of the Dead and then, on a thousand nights, walked into the earth and searched its shadows—if all this were to happen to my hands, would I be Arjuna?' the boy asked himself. 'Would I be he who rescues the princess from Yama's kingdom and brings her back?'"

The boy's stories were those of an imagination suited to a shadow theater; and the boy was, by temperament, suited to a life separated from others by a translucent screen.

The old *dalang* nodded, for what the young man said was true. He would become Arjuna and also Rama and Sinta, Gatotkaca and the Monkey King. He would become the Pandavas and the Kauravas, both. He would give voice and movement to the multitude of men, women, gods, and monsters set down in the crowded pages of the *Ramayana* and the *Mahabharata*.

Sitting in that room invaded by night so that he was like the blind king Dhritarashtra, he saw, nonetheless, the boy's destiny. And in his mind only he said to him, "Yours will be a life enriched by a fabulous dream, and it will be—just as surely—an unhappy one."

The old man knew that Guntur could not be warned against this, his destiny; nor would he change anything in his life to elude it.

As a *dalang*, Guntur would be, like the boy who fathered him, a shadow—a ghost—a teller of stories about shadows and ghosts to people who will be shadows and ghosts for him always. This was his destiny. Storytelling was already written on his heart.

The old man knew all this and said nothing. All that he did say, in the morning as he was preparing to leave the workshop with the teak box containing his new *wayang*, was: "Do you wish to be my apprentice?"

Guntur agreed at once and—after taking ceremonious leave of his father, whom he would see only once more in this world—left for Surakarta with the *dalang*.

12.

To become another—even if only a puppet—is impossible for all but a few. The solitary one not bound to others may sometimes slip from himself like a boat its mooring. It is a paradox of identity that those most absorbed in themselves are most readily transformed. Perhaps to be thought of by others is to be fixed, is to have our identity given by them, is—in the language of the *batik* clothmakers—to have our pattern drawn. Guntur's pattern was a storyteller's. Beyond this, it had not been drawn. Attaining mastery of his *wayang* theater, he might come to inhabit its characters. The man who loved shadows might mingle his own with those cast by his puppets, which are themselves the shadows of stories.

To attain this mastery required an arduous apprenticeship.

From his nineteenth until his twenty-eighth year, Guntur lived in Surakarta, in central Java, as the *dalang*'s apprentice.

During the first year, he did not touch a puppet.

To begin his apprenticeship, Guntur studied the *Ramayana* and the *Mahabharata* and their metamorphoses into stories suitable to Java. The ancient Hindu stories had been altered by the features of the island, by Buddhism and Islam, and by Java's own princes and heroes. Steeping himself in them, Guntur was changed as water is by tea or indigo leaves. The patterns of the great histories concerning the coming of time out of timelessness, the origins of gods and men and monsters—these were drawn onto the apprentice until by the fifth year they were as familiar as his own history. Their lives crowded out his own and what little remained of himself seemed inconsequential. In this way, his power to transform himself into someone else strengthened.

As water in a broken cup drains out into something else, so did Guntur's being flow into the *wayang*. But the power to inhabit perfectly the forms of his art was not his until long after Candra's first death, when the puppet master was in his middle age.

In his apprenticeship's second year, Guntur learned to handle the puppets—to make them walk, skulk, war, dance, or woo according to their nature and story. He had many bad habits to unlearn; his previous handling of the *wayang* had been according to his own pattern, not the theatrical tradition's.

"You must forget yourself," the master *dalang* told Guntur.

It was not until his fourth year that Guntur forgot technique; that is, he no longer needed to consider it, any more than we do walking, skulking, warring, dancing, or wooing if such is our pleasure. The puppets' movements were now his own. He possessed them and they him in the same way that water is shaped by the cup it fulfills.

"When Java fell under the sway of Islam, to look on a puppet as on any representation of the human form was forbidden," the master said. "This is the reason for the white screen kept between the *wayang* and the people who come to see the play, so that they may see only the puppets' shadows. On the *dalang*'s side of the screen is the spirit world, invisible to all but himself. Ours is a world of ghosts."

In his sixth year, Guntur mastered the *gamelan* orchestra. He could conduct it and the *rebab* musician with his eyes and with his body. The musicians were for him like the puppets—instruments of the stories' own mysterious will. He had learned that it was the stories that the *wayang* theater served. They would become preeminent in Guntur's mind.

"You must remember to come back," the old man said. "The shadow world is seductive. You must remember always that you are sitting just outside the door to the Land of the Dead. On the opposite side of the story-screen—that is where the living sit and watch."

In his eighth year, Guntur no longer *saw* the puppets. He could hold their rods of buffalo horn and send them into the story. He forgot that it was he who was telling it. He listened as if to someone else. He forgot that it was he himself manipulating the puppet rods. Their movement did not seem anymore the result of his hands. It remained only for his mind to fill theirs. When this happened, he would be able to detach himself from the *dalang* sitting crosslegged behind the story-screen, who was himself.

As a drop of water separates from a leaf after rain, Guntur would one day slip away—his consciousness enclosed within a form borrowed from the world of stories.

Puppet and puppet master would become identical but not inseparable. This is the paradox of the master *dalang* and the *wayang* he learns to manipulate with more than skill. Skill alone is not enough although it is more than enough to please the people sitting on the other side of the screen, watching the play of shadows. The master and his puppet are not inseparable, so long as he does not allow himself to be seduced by death. Death unites master and puppet, storyteller and story.

"Do not forget that shadows are without substance," the master told his apprentice. "They are not the lintel or the rafter. Shadows can support Yama's palace, which is itself a shadow, but not this theater, which is so much smaller and poorer than a palace. As you become skillful, you may tempt yourself to believe in the substance of the shadows you yourself create. But consider the shadow that falls on the sea from a boat or a seabird hovering in midair. It takes only the wind to make that shadow disappear."

"Does it go inside the water?" Guntur asked. "Does the shadow remain in the sea?"

"I do not know." The old man looked into the corner of the room, at the shadow there, and said: "Death has its fascination, and shadows are nothing. You must remember that."

In the ninth year of Guntur's apprenticeship, the *dalang* gave him his theater and then went to Semarang, where he had been born next to the Java Sea, and there he prepared to die.

"I am satisfied," he said as he was lifted onto a palanquin that would carry him from Surakarta to the sea.

13.

To tell of Guntur's life in Surakarta is to speak of night.

He was like the sky before rain when, at four o'clock, the oil lamp was extinguished and the *wayang* put away after a performance that had begun at eight the night before. Sleep was impossible; and he wished, for a while, to leave the theater and walk through the village streets. Guntur was like a sky that has for too long held its rain and now must release it or be rent by fire.

As he walked, his ears rang with the *gamelan's* music. Because of its accompaniment, the scenes he saw everywhere around him were like those of a play's. And the few people he saw at this hour before the sky began to lighten were like characters in a play. And in his mind, Guntur was Arjuna—his favorite of the Pandavas—whose name means silver, or shining. He did not ask himself why one who lived his life among shadows should assume the role of the shining warrior and friend of Lord Krishna, when he left the theater. But it was so.

Is it not often the case that we are drawn to our opposite and find there our missing self?

Guntur walked with the air of one who has been ennobled, because for as long as he heard the *gamelan's* music in his mind, he was Arjuna—son of Kunti and Indra, king of the demi-gods. Guntur looked around him with the clarity given those who see each action as if through a story's lens or—to use the language of the *batik*-makers—through a pattern whose perfection it is impossible to increase or alter.

Guntur was not always content to be someone else. The puppet Arjuna—he knew—was the shadow of a shadow cast by a form whose shape no one knew, whose origin lay before the first story. To look backward was to become sick with a recession of Arjunas—each one growing paler, smaller, and more a matter of conjecture.

His former master had adjured Guntur to forget himself and also to remember to return to himself. Guntur knew that he must live a portion of his life where people come and go. He might wander from himself, like the Pandavas from the center of the world into the desolate places of their banishment, as long as he returned. And so at the end of each night's performance, he went into the street. But he was uneasy and seldom remained there after first light.

Once, when morning had harried him back to his theater before he had rid his ears of the *gamelan*'s music, he destroyed many of his puppets. That morning Guntur had hated Arjuna, which is to say that he hated himself for being always someone else. As he stood with the ghosts on his side of the story-screen with the thin light falling between the rafters, he felt how unendurable his solitude had become and wept.

Weeping, he tore the *wayang* to pieces and

trampled them. Arjuna, he put into the fire.

He wept in grief at his own nothingness.

That night he closed the theater and traveled to Malang, to his father's workshop. But Guntur could find no way to speak of his sorrow. He might have spoken of himself as a character—told his father the story of his life in Surakarta; but having rebelled at the premeditation of a storytelling where all outcomes are known, Guntur had no form with which to tell his life, or—more accurately—how he had lost it.

His father was uncomfortable and relaxed only at nightfall, after his son had gone out. Guntur recognized no one, though many of those he had known in his childhood lived there still. Although *gamelan* music did not accompany him through the dark streets of his youth, the people he saw seemed to be wearing painted leather masks.

After three days, Guntur ordered new puppets to replace the ones he had destroyed and returned to his *wayang*—a word meaning both theater and puppets.

In Surakarta, he again took up Arjuna, believing that he might find in the son of Kunti and Indra a representative. Guntur was not so lost that he did not see the deception he was practicing on himself. But he was powerless to resist.

"Death has its fascination," his master had told him.

14.

Guntur liked to sit in the market and listen to the voices coming and going in the dark. He felt an attachment to the men and women who arrived before the sun was up, with fish, chickens, ducks, birds, fruit, shells, and flowers to sell. For them he felt affection, if so slight a relationship as this can be called by a word promising so much to the desolate heart.

He sat by the bird catcher's stall and listened to the birds and to a flute playing somewhere by the river, which at this hour was blacker even than night. Each morning that he went outside to be away from the mutely clamoring *wayang*, he listened for that flute—finding in its rough, unskillful melody an artlessness to rid his mind of the *gamelan*'s importunate music. Only then, could he forget a while the stories that ravished him and which he now hated.

He never left the bird catcher's stall to seek out the flute player. It was enough to hear him. That music, with its sinuous line of unfinished notes, wound through Guntur like a coarse cotton thread through a silken tapestry. Its homely purpose, which might have been nothing more than to accompany the grinding of the flute player's morning coffee or to send to the ferryman's daughter his love, pleased Guntur. Listening, it was as if he went in the bird catcher's cart to his hut in the forest and sat at a table of wooden planks to eat a plain meal of rice and sweet potato with the man and his family.

The flute's song enchanted Guntur and emptied him, if for only a few hours, of his ambition. He was ambitious—wanted to be the greatest of all Java's masters of the *wayang*—even as he wished he had never held a puppet rod.

Is this not always so?

But Guntur had spent too many years in the theater, performing the elaborate puppet plays to the exclusion of all else to turn onto some other path.

After listening to the flute player's song, he would sometimes go to one of the women who lived near the market and lie with her in the darkness. His fingers would stroke her with a subtlety that gave intense pleasure. Guntur would move her with the incomparable skill of a puppet master to an ecstasy she seldom experienced in her trade with other men.

Not that it was always the same woman with whom Guntur made what love he was able, for he had no preference and took behind the curtain whatever woman first presented herself. Each of them in that house hoped that she would be the one this time to receive Guntur when he came with the carters and was jealous as such women rarely are.

Guntur lay in the darkness with this one or that and thought nothing of the pleasure he gave, or took. He took little, in fact—only what is necessary to restore a man's balance and temper. He never shared the raptures of the women, who were careful not to confess their exultation to him for fear he would withhold it out of spite or use his power somehow to his advantage. The women of that house understood men, having seen them always when they were most themselves.

Guntur neither lost himself nor found himself in any of the women. The little self that belonged to him remained in him—a hard ball, the pit of a fruit, a stone. Because the soil of his affectionate nature was barren, nothing flowed into the vessel of another. The paradox of losing oneself in another in order to enlarge and enrich one's own being did not occur. He released his seed and thought how like his theater was this house. He lay in the wavering shadows cast by the oil lamp, on one side of a cotton screen while on the other, other men waited their turn.

Guntur would not have entered a woman if desire had not, from time to time, risen up to overmaster him.

He would leave the house while the sky was lightening and walk to a stand in the market for coffee before going home to sleep.

Once, as Guntur sat, enjoying the odor of coffee and of cinnamon that the sudden morning wind carried from the groves, a Portuguese sailor told him the story of Orpheus and Eurydice.

15.

The sailor said:

"The islands of the archipelago are countless, and one of them is the Island of the Dead. This was told to me as I am telling you it now, by a sailor from Messenia, whose ship had been blown wide of its course by a typhoon. It wandered many months among the islands on its return to Singapore. Somewhere on the sea between Malay and the Riau Islands, the crew heard music drifting like a curtain of rain across the water and smelled cinnamon as surely as we do the spiced morning air. In a little while the ship crossed the horizon—a thing not possible for the living—and came into an ocean, which was endless but at the same time ended in a wall of green jasper, raised up into the roof of the sky. There were no clouds, and the sky was not blue but a color impossible to describe in Greek, Portuguese, Malay, or in any other language. The music was falling like rubies and emeralds, like motes of sunlight onto the water.

"They were not afraid.

"The helmsman let go the tiller. The sails were left, unreefed, to the wind. The ship scudded across waves like liquid jade—flew over that green sea into a bay ringed by a pink coral reef—coming to rest a little way from the shore. The spellbinding music was loud—not loud—audible, though it had always been so or how could the crew have heard it? No, not audible—*visible* in the particles of sunlight. They could not say what the music was like—not those men with ordinary senses.

"I cannot tell you what it was like any more than the Greek could tell me," the Portuguese said in Guntur's language.

"The crew rowed to the island—all but the man from Messenia, who was ordered to stay aboard. He would have gone with them in the boat—wanted to go as much as they all did—but was ordered to stay behind and guard the ship.

"The Greek knew, somehow, that it was the Island of the Dead, lying in a mist on the other side of the bay, and that none of them would return; and yet he wished himself with them. I was a young sailor when he told me this story, and I have looked—on and off—for that island ever since."

Guntur asked the Portuguese why he sought it, if to find it meant never to return.

The sailor answered:

"To find my own wife, who died while I was at sea."

And then the sailor told Guntur the story of Orpheus and Eurydice—how Orpheus went to the Underworld and would have brought her back if he had not turned round to see if she were following him.

"When I find the island where my wife is I will blind myself," he told Guntur. "What does it matter so long as I can have her with me."

Guntur was moved by what the Portuguese had told him. It was the first story Guntur had heard that had not been written in the *Ramayana* or the *Mahabharata*, or—in the language of the *batik* clothmakers—drawn already on the world. As he walked to his theater, he was still within its spell; but after he had slept and wakened once more to the enchantment of his own ghosts and shadows, he forgot it.

Guntur undressed in the corner of the theater where he slept, just as the early light claimed for day its temporary dominion. He slept and dreamed *The Abduction of Sinta*, which he would perform that night.

16.

Again, Guntur wondered at the power of the flat, leather puppets to represent the Pandavas, Kauravas, Arjuna, Krishna, Rama, Sinta—all the men, women, gods, and demons of the teeming Hindu stories. He wondered by what magic or art *wayang kulit* had become the visible forms of primordial energy. Only by that energy's numinous light could so poor an object as those puppets have cast its millennial shadow onto the story-screen. The oil lamp was too weak an instrument for the reenactment of creation.

Because Guntur hated the puppets to the degree that he was enthralled by them, he wondered if there could be a theater without them. Might he not sit crosslegged on the floor—without the oil lamp, without the *wayang* and the musicians, without even an audience—sit with arms folded, in silence, and wait for those ancient atoms to travel from the beginning of the world and fall, like a benison, on the white screen? It would be a theater of light instead of shadows, and Guntur would be its solitary master.

Guntur wished he could destroy the origin of the *wayang* itself—the Hindu stories, which bound him to their iron forms. Imagining it gave him a malicious pleasure, as a child imagines his happiness in killing his mother or father, brother or sister, and executes his wish on his toys instead. But were Guntur to deny them, might not Arjuna and the rest rise from their border kingdom to drag him by the hair, compelling him to take up once again the visible warrants of their existence? Although Guntur followed the Lord Buddha and was indifferent to the Hindus' gods, he was not a fool to risk the consequences of desecration.

He sat crosslegged behind the screen—on the side reserved for the *dalang* and his ghosts—and studied the puppets ranged along the green trunk taken from a banana tree. He understood that he was in thrall to them as surely as they were to the stories their shadows enacted. Pity welled up in him for his puppets, from the inexhaustible spring of his own solitude.

"We are ghosts," he murmured as if to a child or a lover. "We are shadows of great events, which happened thousands of years before either of us were made."

He took up Arjuna, his favorite. This Arjuna, which was different and also the same as that one destroyed in the puppet master's iconoclastic fury.

"I'm sorry to have thrown you into the fire," he said.

Setting "the bright one" in the banana trunk, Guntur called for the *rebab* player.

"Tonight we are playing *The Abduction of Sinta*," he told the man, who already knew it. "Shall we practice?"

The musician nodded, sat down on his mat, and began to tune the two strings of his instrument while Guntur took up the Monster King and worked the puppet rods to test the limberness of the joints. Satisfied, they began.

The rods clicked in Guntur's hands while he told how Prince Rahwana, disguised as an old man, abducted Sinta from the forest, where she and Rama were happy despite their banishment, to his kingdom Alangkadiraja. After a lengthy recitation, Guntur signaled with his mallet an adjournment to the action, and the *rebab* accompaniment abruptly ceased. Silence unfurled like a shadow. In it, the puppet master heard the sound of two pieces of wood striking one against the other. He stepped from behind the screen—Rahwana in his hands—to see who had entered the theater.

A young woman stood in the dusky space, light

falling through the small windows, making her black hair shine. She stood, silent and abashed by the master's presence. Guntur said nothing—his own eyes shying away from hers.

"Do you have any puppets to sell?" she asked at last. "For *batik* patterns?"

"Come tomorrow!" he snarled so that she stepped back and the two bangles sounded again on her arm.

He turned abruptly and went behind the white cotton screen.

17.

He could not recall her face.

But the sound her bangles had made remained with him. It was for him an incantation summoning a desire that, until now, had been hidden from him. Guntur did not desire the women he lay with in the house by the market. That which impelled him to seek out a woman was only an agitation of atoms that required calming—a clamor needing to be silenced. What had driven him into women's arms (in the dark they were indistinguishable) was like the hunger for bread that a man will appease by gnawing on a root still dirty from the earth. Guntur's desire for Candra, however, was sumptuous. Centered in his imagination, it was concocted of scent, silk, and a skin comprised of the dark, fragrant, and soft essences of the night.

After the performance as he wandered the town's

empty streets (they, like him, spellbound by a mystery partially revealed in moonlight), he could not recall the young woman's face. Nor could he do so when he lay beside another in the dark nor, later still, in his own room where he experienced torment until this night unknown to him. But he heard in his mind the resonant sound of her two bangles (more resonant than the sound of his mallet's striking to signal the end of a scene). That resonance contained for him a fragrance, softness, a darkness that would have—during the many years Candra was lost to him—the power when he heard it to invoke her. It was—that commonplace sound, little more than noise—the particularity of his love.

His eyes had not rested on her long enough to form anything but an unsatisfactory impression. He had glanced at her face and body—his eyes startled by her sudden appearance in the room. His glance had been fugitive. He had not had presence of mind to *look* before hurrying behind the cotton screen to hide himself. He would not see her face and have time to draw it on his heart until he had rescued her, as Rama did Sinta from Rahwana's castle.

He had noticed her blue hands, but many women who worked for the clothmaker had hands dyed blue, or red, or even gold if they worked with gold lead used to make ceremonial *prada* cloth.

He knew she was beautiful. Is this not the way of love stories? This story is an unhappy one. We know

45

already that Guntur will lose Candra. Soon, it will be her abduction I will recount. We are not in the least surprised to hear that, in five days, she will be dead and Guntur stricken by grief almost past enduring. What surprises is what comes after her first death and his first sorrow.

Guntur got up from his turbulent bed, having slept only a short while. That brief sleep was marred by a nightmare he could not—waking—bring to mind. None of it, except the jarring of a nightbird and the rough, unfinished music of the flute, remained. The sound of the woman's bangles soon replaced them, and Guntur embroidered several amorous daydreams in which they figured, accompanied by his sighs.

Is this not love? But how love, when he had not seen her face or any other part of her clearly? How could love have flamed up in him with the suddenness of a wildfire when he had seen her imperfectly and had heard her ask only the single question broken by her diffidence: "Do you have any puppets to sell? For *batik* patterns?" Are we to believe that the mere sound of one wooden bangle falling against another is enough to incite love?

Yes.

For Guntur, love was stories. He knew hundreds of love stories set down hundreds of years—a thousand years—earlier. He knew well how to intone the voices of lovers: ardent, jealous, peremptory, supplicating, and tyrannical. He could speak love in the timbre of men and of women, of gods and monsters. He could sing love, weep love, and bitterly lament it.

Guntur understood yearning as a map-maker does a hill's voluptuousness or a merchant the abacus's beads that answer to his fingers' caress. For one who spent his life entirely among men, Guntur's knowledge of passion—of affection, even—was untainted by either passion or affection. He would have loved Candra purely had he not loved her excessively. It was adoration—not the desire to possess—that made his love impure.

Impurities in metal ore produce a gorgeously colored flame when put in the metal-worker's fire, but the enchantment is brief and the metal weakened. It is the same with an extravagant passion.

But not for a while yet would Guntur's regard for Candra increase into a dangerous obsession. For now and for the five remaining afternoons she would visit him, Guntur moderated his emotion. Or to be exact, emotion—having been kept circumspect by his inexperience—moderated the rush of invention that unsettled and delighted his imagination. An imagination curbed by the orthodoxy of his art.

He could not recall her face, but it did not matter; it shone in his mind and would continue to shine there even were she to grow old and be no longer beautiful. Her face for him was like the moon, whose light persists in the mind long after one had forgotten its features—whether revealed, or partially hidden as though it had turned its face to look elsewhere.

Is this not also love? Yes, and fanaticism. In his

sudden hunger, he would have gnawed on a root still dirty from the earth, which had clenched it.

Two bangles can compose a love song. A single bangle can be enough to remind a lover of his love.

Guntur washed and prepared for his.

SHADOWPLAY

PART TWO

1.

"Tell me your name," he said to her through the white screen.

"Candra."

"Where were you born?"

"In Tayu, by the Java Sea."

"I do not know what the sea is like," he said, leaning closer to the cotton fabric separating them to see her better. "Tell me."

"Blue."

"I know that. Something else."

He brought his eyes closer still to the screen so that his face nearly touched the cotton. But though he squinted in an attempt to resolve the diffuse image of the young woman's face, he could see it only imperfectly, as *wayang* are seen by those watching a play on the other side of the screen; or as the moon is, reflected in black water creased by the wind. Resigned, he leaned back again and resumed the *dalang*'s crosslegged position behind the green banana trunk bearing his puppets upright by their jointed rods.

She said:

"It seems to end where the sky comes down and rests—a trembling line far off. But always when the boat approaches, it falls away and always there is another far-off line under the sky. Another sky or the same. The wind shakes the sea's distant edge and beats the water white all around us. And when there are also clouds, their shadows roll across the sea like water buffalo stampeding in and out of sunlight. Sometimes flying fish run over the water as we sail toward the horizon, which we must cross to find anchovies—only we never do cross it; always it lies there trembling against the blue or gray sky. Before sunrise or at night, the sea is even more beautiful although it's invisible—except for a circle of moonlight rocking always before us as we sail toward the open water or, at the end of the day, away from it toward land. Then, the sea is something to smell and to hear."

Guntur fell silent—his thoughts in suspension as he waited to hear again the sound of her bangles. But she sat on her side of the screen, without moving—in the stillness of a happiness remembered, of a vision almost beatific in its power to enforce on her silence.

The words are wrong, for what Candra had invoked in the hot dusk of the theater, in the middle of an afternoon, did not demand an obedience she would not willingly give. Her memory of her days and nights on the water was a silken bond such as ties together two lovers who wish only to tighten it. Her childhood was indelible like the dye that transformed her hands into those of a goddess.

Guntur did not think of her hands. He did not think of her face, for he had made up his mind that it was beautiful. He did not think of her form beneath the brown sarong. The bodies of women were no more to him than they are to any man who avails himself of them—or say instead, no more than the hill covered in grass is to the man who wanders it at will; or the sea, to the sailor careless of tempests and Barbary pirates. Neither did Guntur think of Candra's mouth, which he would have liked to taste. He thought of her as a place where he might dwell and escape, at least for a while, his own terrible sway and that of his shadow puppets.

Is this not an artist's fate: to be attracted and repelled by the things of his art and by his own nature, which requires his submission to a vocation that, ultimately, ruins him?

Guntur listened for her bangles striking like mallets against each other but heard only his own breathing and—among the rafters—the rattle of a wasp.

"Tell me a story!" he commanded, having become angry.

"I don't know any," she answered with an absoluteness that made him doubt her.

"Tell me a story," he said—this time without enjoining her to answer.

He heard her shift on her side of the screen and heard the bangles falling together on her arm.

"I've left Ganesha for you on the table," he said gently. "It's yours—I want no money. Say—if you like—that I took what they gave you to buy a *wayang*. Tell them I have others to sell."

He listened while she rose from the floor and went to the table for the Elephant God. She was—in her movements—musical, and he was transported by the sound of her walking in the same way a blind man would be to hear his lover enter the room.

"Come tomorrow with a story, and I'll give you another," he called after her.

2.

Candra did not consider it strange that Guntur had spoken to her through a cotton screen. He was a *dalang* and not an ordinary man. Who knew what proprieties he might have been bound to observe by a profession as mysterious to her as that of a Hindu *guru* or a monk of her own Buddha's. Candra was a simple woman—scarcely more than a girl—a fisherman's daughter, someone who made dye from indigo leaves, molasses sugar, and lime, who knew little of the visible world and nothing of the invisible over which Guntur, as mediator between its shadowy presences and the beings on her side of the screen, presided.

She was young and did not give Guntur (whom she had seen in spite of his hurry to hide himself) any thought at all. Guntur was then forty years old—twice her age and in her eyes already old.

She returned to the clothmaker with Ganesha, stood at her vat until the day's work was finished, and then went home to her aunt's house.

Only that night as she lay waiting for sleep did Candra think about the shadow master—not of him, but his questions. Remembering her description of the sea, she fell back to her childhood and relived her happiness for a second time that day before sleep possessed her.

She pushed the boat out past the churning waves and climbed inside. She undid the sail and felt the boat jump over the water—the water like ruts beneath the hull. She went on toward the horizon, paying out the line by which she could find her way to shore again. That is a storyteller's description of how Candra let go her hold on wakefulness and reason and went beyond the place where she had closed her eyes.

She paid out the line by which she could find her way back to morning and her room.

In the morning as she washed and put on the

brown sarong, she remembered she must visit the theater and tell the shadow master a story.

"But what story can I tell?" she asked herself.

She forgot her obligation to the *dalang* until she was eating fish and rice at midday; the fish recalled for her the sea and the sea the boy who had been her friend in Tayu. She remembered the sea sweeping over the beach—its jade edge breaking on the uneven sand. There, she and the boy would search for nautilus and amphora shells and tell each other stories about people on the sea bottom or on a far island across the sun's doorway into day.

The beach, which might be yellow, pink, or black.

Candra put down her bowl of anchovies and rice and recalled the stories she and the boy would invent, having known then few others.

In Java, hundreds of stories are told—from the *Ramayana* and *Mahabharata*, the *Gita*, *Koran*, *Sutras*, and Scriptures brought to the islands by Portuguese missionaries and, later, by the Dutch and the English. Where so many stories are known and each day told, there is little need of invention. People compare events in their own lives to those in the great tales. If Anwar loses everything through his imprudence, his father will talk of Yudhishthira, who was cheated of his kingdom, brothers, wife, and his own self in a game of dice. If Anwar must escape to Borneo or Sumatra because he cannot pay his debt, the father recounts for us the exile of the Pandavas. The ancient stories are like towering trees in whose shadows only small things can take hold. Knowing few of them, Candra and the boy were like green and scarlet birds singing from the branches their own private songs.

Or like nautilus and amphora shells forgotten on the beach by the rolling ocean.

"I'll tell the old man about the girl who went to an island," she said to herself. "An island beyond the sea's trembling edge where the sky rests."

3.

Candra's story impressed Guntur no more than if it were the remnant of a dream encountered in sleep or fever. What could a *dalang*—master of the storyteller's art—make of a caprice with no other reason for being than her desire to make it so? What effect could such a telling have on one who had not yielded to fancy since he was a boy playing artlessly with puppets?

For Guntur, the world was as a palace is to the king's steward. None of its rooms holds secrets: the least chair or spoon is familiar. But outside its walls, all is not so familiar—may be, in fact, a mystery. Guntur knew the remote corners of Java's sacred imagination, but the young woman's story—alien to it—discomfited him. Inflexible, his mind could not admit a story unhallowed by a thousand years of repetition.

Had he known that his own shadow master

had spent his final weeks in forgetting, that he had emptied himself on his deathbed of all voices save those spoken outside his window by the sea (which suggested to him themes and motives of a harrowing beauty)—had Guntur known that his teacher had surrendered to an elemental nature and made of it a hymn entirely his own, he might have appreciated Candra's invention. But because he had not seen how the old *dalang* entered, finally, a limitless sea, Guntur dismissed her story.

Ten years were to pass until he thought of it again.

Having dismissed it, he asked to hear instead about her life in the village. He found ordinary life strange, though Gandari's having given birth to a stone impressed him not at all. Now, listening to Candra, it was as if he were visiting places in his mind forgotten or never guessed at.

She told him this:

"I wake when the room begins to lighten, wash, and dress. I grind coffee beans. With my aunt and uncle, I eat fruit, bread, and drink coffee. I go to work at the clothmaker's, stirring leaves in a wooden vat. At midday, I eat rice and fish, or rice and chicken. I make more dye. I go home and help my aunt cook dinner. We eat, and I wash the pots. I walk to my friend Liat's house by the river, or I sit in the yard of my aunt's house until night comes and with it the stars. I undress, wash myself, and go to sleep."

Always before that afternoon, the supernatural had cast its shadows onto the story-screen. Now it was the familiar world, borne on Candra's voice, that entered the shadow world thronged with ghosts. Had Guntur held the white cotton screen to an otherworldly light, he might have seen particles of gold caught in the weave, left there by the costly *prada* cloth worn by gods and warriors. Had he held it up to that light, he might have seen radiant traces of the bright one himself—Arjuna, whose chariot was driven by the Lord Krishna. Charged by energies that for so many years had entered the visible world through it, the story-screen now had power to intensify and exalt the ordinary into the extraordinary. As Candra spoke to Guntur of her life, its mundane and meager aspects nonetheless shone in his mind. To this extent did Candra's voice move Guntur nearly to awe.

Nearly?

Awe was impossible for someone who invoked the forms of omnipotence with nothing but buffalo leather or goatskin, smoothed by a glass bottle, and enacted ancient dramas illuminated by an oil lamp.

Did Guntur love Candra?

Yes.

What quality of love?

He loved her according to one of love's multifarious forms, which include the perverse and the cruel.

What of desire?

He desired to possess—not her body, but her being; to annex her life to his and to the stories by which his life was constituted; to incorporate her ordinary life (having first intensified and exalted it) into the vast confluence of extraordinary stories that formed him; to install her among his familiars in one of the palace rooms.

By his own idea of her was he captivated. The fragrance of the cinnamon trees, which the wind had gathered and carried into the theater with her, became her fragrance. The image of her face, softened and blurred by the cotton screen, persisted like a bright color does when the gaze is turned elsewhere. That altered image became the face he saw always when he thought of her and even—much later—when he saw her without the story-screen between them. It appeared also behind his closed eyes when he lay down to sleep; and it mingled with the phantoms of his dreams.

The rough music of her bangles heard whenever she raised or lowered her arm became the musical accompaniment of his love's story.

He did not know that the sound her bangles made signified her annoyance at this old man who tried to seduce her. And he meant to seduce her with the clothmaker's money given her to buy *wayang*. Money she wanted so that she might buy some pretty blue *batik* for a dress to wear to the wedding of her friend.

A blue cloth to match Candra's hands.

She came each afternoon and answered Guntur's questions through the screen, her bangles clicking angrily.

"Where were you born?" he asked.

"In Tayu, by the Java Sea."

"I do not know what the sea is like."

"I told you before: it is blue!"

Click clack.

"I was—" and he told her about his life in Malang with his father and, later, in Surakarta with the old *dalang.*

She sat and waited for him to let her go out into the sunlight. She hated the theater with its shadows that seemed to cling to everything in it like ants to sap from the *tinggi* tree. Shuddering, she would rub her arms and legs as if to wipe the sticky shadows from them.

Click clack.

She hated the silence, broken only by Guntur's rising and falling voice, by the rattling of a wasp among the rafters, and by her bangles. She longed to be away from there—even if it were only to stand at her vat and mix with a paddle indigo leaves, molasses sugar, and lime.

"What is your house?" he asked when he had finished a portion of his history.

"The third," she said.

"Come tomorrow," he said.

She took Sugriva, the Monkey King, from the table and fled.

4.

When Candra thought of Guntur, it was at night as she lay on her mat, waiting for sleep. For her, his theater was an island of shadow surrounded by a sea of light. But when the light went out of the sky, the shadow rolled like a cloud's over the face of the waters, engulfing the village and her house. It was as if the shadow master had let down a bridge separating him from ordinary men and women in order to slink like a demon into the night, which is the commingling of all shadows. Then, Candra was afraid, lying in a darkness relieved by a spangling of stars.

She could not recall Guntur's face any more than he could hers. Her eyes had been on the floor between them that first afternoon when she had surprised him holding Rahwana in his hands; and during the five ensuing afternoons, the story-screen had been between them. In the darkness of her room invaded by dank river smells, Guntur would come unbidden to her mind. His face was as a piece of that darkness—a smudge like one left carelessly on the wall by her uncle after having adjusted the wick of a smoking oil lamp.

This night (the sixth after she had first gone to the theater to buy *wayang*), Gatotkaca lay on a palm leaf in the corner of her room. Dizziness had seized Candra as she had hurried from the theater into the afternoon—eyes stung and momentarily blinded by the overwhelming light. She had had to lean against the door jamb to keep from falling, the warrior puppet held weakly by the rod in her hand. A languor and nausea had followed, which kept her from returning to the clothmaker to give the *batik* copyist her newest acquisition.

Candra had gone immediately to bed, closing her eyes against the late afternoon light and the pitching motion, which made of her mat a boat on which she set out for an island beyond the sunrise. She imagined Gatotkaca was with her—his strong hand on the tiller—a warrior descended from giants and possessed of supernatural power. This, Guntur had told her when she had taken the puppet from the table, before hurrying into the dazzling afternoon.

"Hurry!" she cried to the warrior who, no longer a *wayang*, stood gigantically in the space created by her fever—his immense godlike head wreathed in clouds. "The shadow is spreading over the water," she said in her delirium. "If it touches us, we'll die."

Sail fat with wind, the boat flew eastward—flushing from the sea's moving hills flying fish, whose stiff wings rattled like those of wasps or like locusts, which fell every seven years on the green fields and devoured them. The boat flew toward a sun streaming red and orange flame as it dragged itself slowly from the water. The boat flew as if Gatotkaca willed it—he who had the secret of wingless flight and was ally to Arjuna and his brothers in the war of the Pandavas and the Kauravas.

But always Guntur's shadow rolled after the boat, blackening the sea behind it the way a storm will, which mariners will struggle to outrun, having let out the sails uselessly. The waves blackened and seemed to stand still, frozen like those of the polar seas beneath an avalanche of darkness.

Frozen, the waves—the sea's many tongues, which give voice to its stories.

Candra shivered as Guntur's vast shadow slipped up the sides of the boat and poured in blackly to the gunwales. She cried out once and was drowned. Rushing into her room, the aunt and uncle found their niece dead—hair and clothes wet, her dry lips tasting of salt had anyone been there to kiss them.

Early that morning, before the sun had dragged itself up from darkness, Guntur prowled the marketplace, unable to sleep. He did not go this time to the house and lie next to one of the women, no longer desiring their bodies or the body of any other woman. He sat in the clamorous night, black sky piled high with celestial houses, and listened to the flute playing by the river. Its unfinished notes bore the sorrow of Candra's uncle.

5.

Not by his body had Guntur hoped to possess Candra, but by words. His words and hers as they passed through the story-screen. Perhaps it was for this reason that he remained on his side of the fabric: so that she might be reduced to a voice. He was a shy man, unused to women except those whom he sought out when desire mounted in him until it could not be ignored. It might have been to mitigate his shyness that he wanted only her voice. But whatever the reason, he wished to ensnare her in his sentences and to be—in turn—caught in hers.

She had been sullen. He had always to coax her to say more. He sensed that she resented him but was helpless against his wish to absorb the story of her days into the compendium of stories with which he understood the world. The monotony of her life was no less surprising to him than the Arctic regions discovered in our own time by Sir John Franklin are to us.

He had not wished Candra harm; her fear of him was, in any ordinary sense, unfounded. But her instinctive dread had been justified by his unrelenting interest; it had struck her as forcibly as a dark cloud passing across the sun does a blind person. She had sat on the floor in the twilit space and listened to him talk and felt his unseen presence stealing over her.

He had said to her:

"My life has been spent among … Not before

have I … Women are to me … My father and the old *dalang* … I was, even when a child, helpless to … hopeless in … I have not … how strange I feel with you, fascinated as if by a flower not seen before, a fragrance … My life before now, my life after now, the days … I am not so very old after all, not so … The sea, how it must … You are like a star obscured until now by morning light … Your voice insinuates itself in me, your words, like seeds, grow up in me, your sentences are like vines entangling me … like *like like!*"

She had said to him:

"My name is Candra. I am twenty-five. I come from Tayu, on the Java Sea. My father is a fisherman. My mother and sister worked in the rice and sweet potato fields. I left them to live with my aunt and uncle. I make indigo dye. I was sent to buy your old puppets. With the money I keep, I will buy some blue *batik* to make a dress for the wedding of my friend. I live with my aunt and uncle in a house near the river. My aunt works for the clothmaker. My uncle is a ferryman. I like to walk to my friend's house in the evening or sit in the yard and watch the coming of the night. My friend's name is Liat. Sometimes I dream of the sea. I would like to see it again."

When she had finished, he asked—like one amazed by a revelation of the uncanny—to hear it again. Each afternoon, the same. And by a paradox of love, the little that she did, in actuality, reveal about her life was made all the richer by the power of his imagination, which had been stimulated into being by Candra and which was increased now by the license he gave it.

She had said nothing about the boy, the shells they had gathered on the beach or her father's anger. Whether she had not thought of them or wanted to keep them for herself—for whatever reason, she had not spoken of them to Guntur. What she had said, however, was enough for a love that asked only for an adjournment to silence. Silence, like dust, reigned in that stillness of dreams and twilight.

Silence and dust laid down by time.

Is it so strange that a man ripe for love—in desperate need of it—should fall in love with the first woman who presents herself? An existence never before guessed at had become the sole object of his regard with the speed of a wildfire sweeping through parched grass. What was strange was the nature of his love.

She might almost have guessed that what Guntur desired was her words. He had wanted to be absorbed in them and to absorb her in his own. He knew a dangerous secret: that the world is made of words. That sun and moon, leaves and dust are words only, and so, too, men and women. Arjuna was words and Ganesha and Sugriva, Guntur's father and the old *dalang* also—only names, and the sentences spun by time's wheel into stories.

When finally she would say no more, Guntur had insisted that she come the next day. She had nodded and snatched up a puppet from the table and hurried outside where the clamor of the people in the dusty street became confused in her mind with the reeling light.

6.

Did Candra die by a contagion of desire? Can such a thing happen?

In a story, it can happen.

Candra perished, then, in the fire of Guntur's passion; his fever became hers in the same way pestilence passes from one person to another. Or as a story is passed from one to another, for stories are another contagion. A week after meeting Guntur, she was dead.

That is how it happened in *The Woman with Blue Hands*, which I saw in a shadow-puppet theater in Cirebon when I was a young man. I was there, in the Dutch army during the Padri War. I had arrived during the famine and left before the typhoid epidemic.

Guntur's love for Candra began one afternoon when she came to buy *wayang*. He yearned for her until she was consumed by his fever and, afterwards, for all the days and nights before his own death by fire. I saw the play with a Dutchman of the East India Company, who told me the story afterwards; I don't understand Javanese. What the *dalang* actually recited and what the Dutchman might have embroidered according to his own fancy, I cannot tell. Nor can I say what in this story may be due to my own secret need.

For five nights, Guntur went out to be alone with the novelty of his sensations. He embraced them as if they were the woman herself. He walked to the river and sat in the shadow of a cinnamon grove, whose fragrance was Candra's. He watched her return from her friend's house or sit motionless in the yard—the bangles quiet on her arm. The sky was a roof under which they both sat, though she did not know Guntur was there inside the darkness of the trees—blacker even than the sky. She looked carelessly at the stars while he looked at her, whose face he could almost see in the light that fell from the window and lay—a yellow oblong—on the grass. When she went into the house, Guntur remained, hoping to see her at the window. He sat on through the night while the stars moved in procession until her uncle left the house to ferry across the river those who brought fish, fruits, flowers, and shells to sell in the marketplace. When Guntur heard the uncle play his flute next to the river, he returned to his theater; for he knew she would be angry to see him.

These were Guntur's thoughts while he sat in the cinnamon grove, beneath the houses of the night (each night recalled later by the puppet he had given Candra during its afternoon).

The first night (Ganesha): "I want only to exist under the same night as Candra, to keep between us this darkness or—in daylight—the white screen."

The second night (Bhishma): "When she sits on the other side of the screen, I sense Arjuna and the rest withdrawing—unwilling to enter the visible world over which she presides for as long as she is there."

The third night (Drona): "I would destroy, again, Arjuna and all the rest of them if she would consent to remain with me. I would set fire to the theater and live in the cinnamon grove if only she would visit me there."

The fourth night (Sugriva): "She is only a girl who stands all day at a dye vat, who knows nothing of the worlds on either side of the story-screen. She scarcely speaks at all, but still do I make of her voice a world greater than any other. I don't understand my desire. It is like hunger in a man who never knew that he was hungry—thirst in someone who did not know he was dying of it."

The fifth night (Gatotkaca): "Standing in the yellow light, she seems a golden statue of Kali, goddess of annihilation."

Much later, when he would take up one or the other of his puppets, it would remind him of some aspect of Candra—the intonation of her voice, her elusiveness, her power to annihilate gods and princes.

When the light began to slant through the trees and the ferryman played in concert with the birds and river his morning song, Guntur hurried to the theater and stayed there as if in quarantine.

Each day his fever increased. He did not rehearse the shadow play to be performed at week's end. The musicians came, and he sent them home. Stopping inside the pavilion to eat what they had brought with them, they were driven away. Grumbling, they went home to discuss with their wives what reason the *dalang* might have for such behavior, while Guntur sat in the doorway to the invisible world or lay sleeplessly on his mat, weaving on the loom of his senses a sumptuous cloth with which to fashion his dream of Candra.

Inside the theater, the instruments of the *gamelan* orchestra were silent. No voice rose and fell, announcing the entry of gods, princes, and demons into the space in front of the story-screen—the visible world into which ghosts appeared by the *dalang*'s intercession. All was silence and dust and the slow passage of time, measured by the daily payment of a puppet to Candra so that she might buy a length of blue cloth. Guntur wept, knowing that no matter how completely the thought of her became part of him (like a ribbon tangled in a bird's nest), it would not be enough—wept, too, because he could no longer be separated from her any more than the ribbon can be from the nest without destruction.

He burned. He burned with desire and, partly, from shame. He wept and railed against his doom.

What was his shame?

That he might be dissembling; that, after all,

the shining thoughts which he had, like a spider, spun in the gloom of his shadow theater might be counterfeit—that what he felt for Candra was closer to the passion of ordinary men, whom he scorned even as he sent out into their gross world the tokens of the sublime. Maybe it was for this that Guntur kept the story-screen between them: so that he would be unable to take her with his eyes—search her sarong for evidence of the sensuousness of her young body.

What was his doom?

To love without reason a woman who belonged elsewhere. To love without caution a woman never intended for him. To make of love a folly, which ruined him. To have squandered his days and nights uselessly. To have seen himself for what he was.

The Woman with Blue Hands is the story of a desire to possess another that trespasses against reason and the order of the world. Even a Dutchman can understand Guntur's offense.

After I had left Java, the typhoid epidemic fell like fire onto the island. Many died of fever. Reading about it in an Utrecht newspaper, I remembered Candra—her story and the fever that had emptied her of all life as a wasp is left a dry husk by fire. It was Guntur who had emptied her—of her words—and who had filled her with his own, which were husks of dead things. *Wayang*, shadows. Ghosts. The *dalang*'s play I had seen in East Java suddenly possessed me

71

with its ghosts. I was captive to its story for reasons of my own.

Having left the army to write pamphlets for the East India Company, I decided to write the story of Guntur and Candra—this shadow play, which I am relating for you now. I wrote as I remembered having seen it in Cirebon and having heard its story told afterwards. I wrote because of a woman I had left long before in Amsterdam, who had died there of fever while I was away in the army. A young woman I had loved, in my way, as fiercely as Guntur did Candra. Only without words. Words came much later to me, when I was no longer young and life was something only to be written about.

7.

Neither on the seventh nor the eighth afternoon did Candra come to the shadow theater. Duryodhana and Abhimanyu lay on the bamboo table for her to snatch up and carry off into the street—noisy with carts at this time of day. Guntur sat waiting behind the white screen, at the doorway to the spectral world.

He was distracted by the creaking wheels of the heavy carts, the shouts of the carters to the merchants who escaped out of their doors the afternoon heat, and by the Portuguese soldiers lounging in the shadows of the shopfronts—faces red and sweating from having drunk too much palm wine. Guntur had never been distracted by everyday life; he could sit all day behind the story-screen with ears cocked for ancient voices, his mind's eye alert to the slightest movement from beyond. Now, he heard those voices indistinctly if at all and saw the bright robes and armor of the Hindu shades as if they were flies on the margin of sight.

Candra never again came to buy a puppet. Duryodhana and Abhimanyu lay together on the table until fire destroyed them.

Guntur's restlessness grew to rage; and no one was foolhardy enough to break down the door, which he had locked, to discover its cause. In his rage, he did not destroy the *wayang* or pull down the linen screen. Why they should have been spared is not known unless the ghosts themselves stayed his hand, knowing that he would need them. Having been excluded from the visible world by the young woman's presence, they returned to cast their shadows on the white partition. Once more, they loved and bickered while Guntur sought in the properties of his theater the consolation of habit. Their wrangling sent him, finally, to his mat and sleep. During the night, the *wayang* stole into his dreams, which were confused and terrifying as if the war between the Pandavas and the Kauravas were being waged in them. Nowhere in them could he find Candra.

In the morning, Guntur dressed and went, without washing, to the clothmaker.

"The young woman who makes indigo dye—

why hasn't she returned to buy *wayang*?" he asked the women standing with their paddles at the dye vats.

"Do you mean Candra?" one of the women asked.

"Yes!"

Thinking that the *dalang* was interested in Candra only as someone who bought his worn puppets, the woman said thoughtlessly: "Last night she died."

Guntur's knees bent and his shoulders sagged like someone who has been given almost too much weight to bear. He could only repeat, stupidly, what the woman had said. He said it in a way that was neither a question nor declaration, irresolutely, while his mind grappled as if bringing from a great depth a secret so that it might be known and understood.

"She came down with fever," she said. Then she went back to her work.

Again, Guntur's shoulders sagged and his knees shook until he could master them. He turned and left without another word to the women at the vats. He moved like an animal for slaughter staggers a step or two after the hammer has struck.

Guntur went into the street and leaned against a tree. For a long time, he stayed there, thinking nothing at all—unaware of the people passing, the sullen oxen and dogs, the *muezzin*'s calling of *adhan*, a dispute between two Sikh traders, a soldier's derision. The afternoon gave way to evening, sunset to night. Only a breeze bearing the odor of cinnamon brought him to himself or, rather, called the young woman to mind.

He walked to her house and crouched in the darkness of the grove. He kept watch as if he expected to see her walk through the yellow light lying on the grass. The yard was empty. No one came or went. All was silent except for the intricate noise of the night.

In the morning, Candra's body was laid on the pyre, dressed in a brown sarong.

8.

The door to the theater remained locked until people began to forget that they had once gone inside to watch shadows woo and war upon the story-screen. So long was the house shut up that it might once have been anything—a temple, granary, or a store whose wares no one could remember. No one knew, either, what the strange and solitary man did inside. Guntur seldom left the playhouse. When he did leave it, he went to buy rice, fish, or fruit. He went at dawn, when the market opened, so as not to be seen and have to give an account of himself. Some believed he had left Surakarta to be a *dalang* in the royal court. A few confused in their minds Candra's death with his. Most forgot him.

How could a man, having seen a woman for so brief a time and that imperfectly through a white cloth, grieve for her so inordinately? Would he, in his grief, retire from the world—cut himself off from what he had known of it before losing her, with the blindness and savagery required for an act of self-mutilation?

Guntur was in love with his *thought* of Candra. (Perhaps for this reason the screen had been always between them.) A bereaved husband will find in the place he shared with his wife a thousand traces of her. He will be stung and finally healed by them, just as salt stings and cures a wound. Nothing of Candra remained in the playhouse—not so much as a strand of hair caught in an ivory comb. What there was of her existed in Guntur's mind. Having no object apart from itself, his mind could not escape the constant stimulus of its anguish. A bereaved husband will press against him his dead wife's dress—his grief for the body that had worn it, inconsolable; later, he will touch the dress fondly, recalling the pleasure he had taken in seeing his wife wearing it. In the end, he will give the dress away or burn it, so that his mind can be relieved of the habit of sorrow. Guntur had nothing to burn, nothing to give away—nothing, therefore, with which to discharge his feeling of desolation.

Unlike an ordinary shrine, which celebrates the god's unseen presence, the shadow theater became a temple to the woman's absence. Shut away in their teak boxes, the *wayang* lay still and silent. The sole ghost was Candra's while time laid down its dust, measuring months then years.

At dawn, Guntur would go to the market to buy some rice, fish, or fruit. He did not ease his torment with the women who made their living in that way. He did not linger anymore under the trees to listen to the coarse humor of the merchants, which once he had liked to do; nor did he heed with pleasure the rough music of the ferryman. If Guntur had done so, he might have heard how the music became, in time, less mournful as the ferryman's grief abated until one morning it vanished altogether. Perhaps that was the morning when he heard from a man who had been in the capital news of an uprising against the Portuguese at Solor. Or maybe it was that the light broken on the water by the morning breeze once more entranced him. For whatever reason, the ferryman's song never again spoke only of sorrow.

Time laid down its dust but could not lay to rest the ghost that haunted the dusky room with the persistence of the wasp rattling among its rafters. The merchants in the marketplace and the man who came to the door to sell Guntur water mistook him for a holy man because of his untended beard and hair and the ragged condition of his clothes.

Except for the story-screen, the theater was empty—the musicians having long before removed their instruments. Had someone gone inside, he would scarcely have guessed that it had been a playhouse—thinking the cotton fabric dividing the room an idiosyncrasy of its melancholy tenant. But almost no one went there. Twice, Guntur allowed a Chinese doctor inside to administer an herbal infusion with properties nicely calculated to restore harmony. Guntur suffered periodically from immoderate sensation—this, in a man who had, for most of his life, been merely a conveyor of shadows.

The *wayang* waited—still and silent inside their boxes; the wasp (always there was a wasp) rattled among the dry rafters; and sometimes the wind carried from the cinnamon grove Candra's fragrance, which made Guntur weep in remembrance.

It does sometimes happen that a person will make of his grief a sanctuary from the world—compiling in a single loss all his grievances against the world. He will make a spiced dish of his sorrow, which he comes to crave more than any other. To say that Guntur exalted his pain would belittle his earnestness, but it is also true that he would not have readily parted from it. He was one of those who live a long time with emotion checked by an unusual intelligence and, when restraints are cast off, become enslaved to emotion.

He had spent only six afternoons with Candra! What store of memory could there be in six afternoons of what was, in essence, an interrogation—his, of her—and monologue—his, to her?

To ask that is to be ignorant of obsession—its extremity, ingenuity, and possessiveness. A single afternoon can sometimes be enough—even a single afternoon of silence.

Think how a dog that discovers a bone in the grass will each day return, even should it never again find a bone there. Is a man any less persevering? Will he not return time after time to a remembered pleasure even if he finds only disappointment and bitter regret?

It is not true that Guntur left the playhouse only at dawn and only to provide himself with necessities. In the months following Candra's death, he had stood each night in the grove just beyond her aunt and uncle's house. He waited with no greater expectation than to see the uncle or aunt. Guntur was greedy for the least crumbs of what might remain in them of Candra, just as *winterkoning*—our Dutch sparrows— taste summer in the crumbled bread they devour on the icy windowsill.

One night, Guntur had gone across the river in the uncle's boat—his face disguised by the strengthening darkness, when the moon has set and the sun not yet risen.

"Why do you play your flute so sadly?" he had asked the ferryman, hoping to hear Candra's name spoken aloud—to hear, possibly, the old man recount the story of his niece as he rowed.

But the uncle had replied, unsatisfactorily, with a question of his own: "Why does a peacock call so mournfully?"

Guntur went on with him to the farther shore in silence and then, as if repenting of his journey, had asked to be rowed back.

It is also true that some months after Candra's death, Guntur had gone to the clothmaker's to beg the aunt for Candra's two wooden bangles. But he was told that the girl had worn them on her funeral pyre, above one of her blue hands.

"They are with her in Paradise," the woman had said to him.

And were her hands really blue?

In the space and time consecrated to myth—legend—to stories surpassing what is given us to know of life, Candra's hands were blue. It is important to this story that they be so, for how else will Arjuna find Candra in the multitude of the dead?

Toward the end of his exile, Guntur opened the teak chests and took out the *wayang*. What could have impelled him to take up the shadow puppets again is not known unless the impulse originated not with Guntur but with the *wayang* themselves. Having been so long silent and still, they might have whispered in a voice that insinuated in Guntur's mind a seduction impossible to resist. For whatever reason, he began to rehearse *The Abduction of Sinta*.

In what place was his exile?

The desert of scorched hope. Or else the forest in which we lose ourselves among our obsessions.

9.

The rods were awkward in Guntur's hands, and the puppets faltered behind the screen. No longer supple, his hands had forgotten how to divine the presence of the unseen. His voice also faltered. It would advance haltingly, as if words were stones above the surface of a river to be crossed with deliberation. During his exile, Guntur had lost the habit of speech. But an uncommon—even unnatural—sympathy for the *wayang* had not lessened during the years he had kept himself apart from people and puppets, both. If anything, it had increased while he taught himself to enter the minds of his puppets, especially that of Arjuna with whom he most identified.

To say that Arjuna or any other of Guntur's puppets had minds is only to suggest the inordinate degree to which Guntur had concentrated his attention on them. Dwelling exclusively on some few objects, the mind may sometimes overcome the distance between itself and them. It will imagine that it is regarding other intelligences when these are, in actuality, only itself. Guntur had held his puppets in mind with so much fervor and fixity that he believed he could possess them where they lay shut up in their boxes. (Unless invisible powers had, in truth, materialized in Guntur's shadow puppets—in which case, they might be said to have minds and with them to have subjugated Guntur's own.)

Guntur would tell stories from the *Ramayana*

and the *Mahabharata*—for months and years he would tell them until they were enacted in the room without need of shadow puppets. Possibly no other *dalang* had ever made a theater of his thoughts alone. When Guntur did finally take the puppets in his hands and once more had mastered them, he was no longer an ordinary *dalang*. His power over the *wayang kulit*, over the stories' gods and demons, princes and warriors—over the time and distances of myth—had no equal. Supernatural powers were now his and sufficient to the journeys he undertook to find Candra.

Night after night, Guntur (in the form of Arjuna) and Arjuna (in the person of Guntur) traveled through all the heavens and hells known to the devout and to the damned. Guntur sat crosslegged behind the story-screen, sounding in his mind the music of the *rebab* and *gamelan*; and in his mind (which was also Arjuna's), he searched the darkness. As Rama had pursued Sinta to Rahwana's castle, so did they now— Guntur and Arjuna—pursue Candra across rivers, over white deserts, and through bleak forests. They went on foot, in boats, and on the backs of elephants. They flew with Gatotkaca, the Flying Knight, above the Sudirman Mountains. Each night they advanced farther, stopping at dawn in exhaustion under a tree, in a cave or a tent erected in the desert against the desert's heat. And when the light was gone once more from the sky, Guntur sat on the floor behind the story-screen and began his journey anew—Arjuna's journey and his own.

The ways leading to the Land of the Dead are not straight. They move, they go forward and double back on themselves. They writhe hypnotically like white snakes of snow before the wind; like certain snakes, they devour themselves. The ways are like carpets taken up at the beginning of summer and laid down in the wrong rooms at summer's end. Demons harry the wayfarers with snares, with fog and confusion. One can arrive in the afterlife by dark or lighted paths, but one cannot always be certain which of the two he has taken or if the path on which he set out is the same as he now finds himself. The ways leading to the Land of the Dead are strange and forbidding, and there is more than one fatal land.

Guntur came to understand that the ways are, in actuality, sentences composing—in his case—the story of his rescue of Candra, which was more difficult than Rama's of Sinta, who had not been ravished by death but by a monster. Prince Rahwana had become enamored of Sinta, the beautiful wife of Prince Rama.

Disguising himself as an old man, Rahwana erased with his own magic the magic circle Rama's brother had drawn round Sinta to protect her in her husband's absence. Rahwana took her by force to Alangkadiraja—his kingdom—and locked her in Alengka, his castle. Aided by the Monkey King, Prince Rama followed the monster and slew him with a magic arrow.

Guntur invoked Sinta's story, hoping to repeat its happy outcome. But he failed. For a hundred nights, he and Arjuna traced her path from the Dandaka Forest, where Sinta and Rama lived out their exile, across the desert and into the mountains of Alangkadiraja. A hundred times they besieged Rahwana's castle, a hundred times broke down Alengka's great door, and a hundred times slew the monstrous prince with magic arrows. But Candra was never there. Candra's story was not Sinta's, and Guntur would not find the young woman in the brown sarong in Alangkadiraja.

At last, Guntur understood that it was his own rising and falling voice, which paved with words the ways to the afterlife. And he remembered the old *dalang*'s admonition against invention for its presumption against the ancient forms of storytelling. But Guntur knew that he had reached the end of all known forms and, like a navigator on the brink of the world, must enter the unknown with neither map nor history to guide him. Like *wayang* that the clothmakers purchase as readymade patterns for the decoration of *batik*, the immemorial patterns of stories, too, can lose their usefulness and serve merely to reproduce an empty form. While it was not uncommon for a *dalang* to improvise (Guntur's and his mentor's condemnation of the practice notwithstanding), the result was limited to a comic or satiric confirmation of reality. Never before this had a *dalang* improvised in order to extend his story—and himself—beyond what was previously known.

Guntur now embarked on other, more formidable journeys from behind the story-screen—to Vaikunth, the heaven of Vishnu; to Kailash, the heaven of Shiva; and to Brahmalok, the heaven of Brahman. With his voice paving the way and with an almost unearthly skill in the manipulation of the *wayang*, he traveled as far as Indralok, where the blessed sit beneath red *parijata* trees. With his radiant shadow puppet, Arjuna, Guntur went also to Yamalok—Lord Yama's infernal palace where Chitragupta pronounces irrevocable judgment on all human souls.

But nowhere among all that dead did Guntur find Candra.

10.

One night Guntur did not go in search of Candra in his theater's limitless shadowland, which might also have been the equally limitless space of his mind. He did not take up Arjuna, did not sit crosslegged on the floor behind the story-screen, did not sound in his mind the music of the *rebab* and the *gamelan*. He lay down on his mat and slept.

And for the first time, he dreamed of the sea.

In his dream, a girl walked into the sea and climbed into a boat just beyond the rolling waves. Having let out the sail, she sat by the tiller and steered toward the place where the sun would soon rise. Guntur knew, in his dreaming, that it was the Java Sea and the girl was

Candra as he had often imagined her. He was dreaming the story she had told him ten years earlier, while she sat on her side of the white cotton screen, so that she might take to the clothmaker a puppet.

The boat flew over the water, accompanied by flying fish which sang a nonsense song to wake the sun. The girl's long hair loosed itself darkly in a morning wind fragrant with cinnamon. And the boat sped toward the horizon even as the sun began to pull itself up from sleep and so, once more, light the world. The black sea lightened, turned gray, then blue. The horizon trembled, and the sea round the boat now resembled a vast indigo cloth, which a wind's rough handling has creased.

The horizon trembled as if in nervous expectation, for the girl was steering a course for it that no power on earth could deflect. Implacably, she was making for the horizon; and contrary to all mortal experience, it did not recede. The horizon line to which she steered remained as if fixed to the spot on the earth's watery bulge where first her eyes had detected it—black against the night's lesser black, with here and there a lingering star. The horizon did not fall back in order to keep between it and the approaching boat a constant distance. Instead, the boat closed on it. And as it did so, the flying fish trilled all the louder, the sky rolled shining and silken overhead, and the sun vanished. Or rather the sun was no longer a flaming disk above the water but an unfolding rose—coral and cinnamon and singing in concert with the fish.

Guntur dreamed that the sea at last stopped its ceaseless motion; the waves lay down and the wind, which had been blowing from every corner at once, uncreased the indigo cloth before returning to its caves at the ends of the earth. Not caves—nautilus and amphora shells.

The boat crossed the blue horizon and entered the sea's far side—the first boat built by human hands to do so. And on it, Candra entered that impossible sea.

Guntur did not dream what happened next; if he did, he forgot it. Or if it was not a figment forgotten upon waking, it was one that the dreaming mind could find neither words, sounds, images, nor fragrances with which to speak of it to the mind's waking half. The girl had entered a place where sensations were perceived only by gods and by the dead—a passageway leading from the visible to the invisible world.

He dreamed further; and what he dreamed, he remembered. Candra at the tiller, the boat drawn up on an island's pink and yellow sand, a coral reef through which the boat had passed and—beyond it—a green jasper sea from which came the odor of cinnamon. Guntur watched her step lightly from the boat and lightly walk across the sand toward countless pavilions in whose radiant shadows the dead were sleeping. Their faces seemed to him like yellow diamonds heaped in the sun, though here there was no sun—only light and music, which were the same. Their faces seemed like lanterns carried at night by the fishing boats, whose lights appear and disappear in the rolling sea's deep troughs. But here, light and dark were indistinguishable—or say, instead, that these and other familiar categories of existence had no meaning.

The pavilions were red, blue, gold, and green silk. The music danced like motes of sunlight on the water.

Guntur woke and recalled on the instant of waking the story of Orpheus and Eurydice told to him long before by a Portuguese sailor. And with the harrowing certainty of one who has endured a revelation, Guntur knew that the island sought by the Portuguese was the same as in Candra's story. Guntur knew where he would find Candra and that he could bring her back, provided he did not turn round to see if she were following him.

11.

There are many stories like this of the Thracian lovers, who believed passion could outwit death. In one told in Japan, Izanagi descends to the Land of the Yellow Stream to bring back from the dead his wife and sister Izanami. But like Orpheus, he fails because of mistrust or impatience. In the *Ramayana* and the *Mahabharata*, the inconsolable also hunt among the shades for lovers ravished by a dark and irresistible desire. But it was the Portuguese's story that had captivated Guntur in some remote region of the mind unlocked only in a dream or by accident. It was by accident that he had learned it while searching the village's shadows for evidence of the ordinary life of men.

Unless it was his destiny and doom to meet a Portuguese sailor and to listen to his story.

Guntur did not ask himself how it was that Candra had imagined an island so like that described by the Portuguese, nor did he wonder how much his dream might have been colored by the sailor's tale. Perhaps she had heard somewhere an echo of the very first story in which the Land of the Dead was to be found—not in the underworld with its mineral light, but in the sea on the other side of an uncrossable horizon.

Where could she have heard it?

From the Java Sea, perhaps, when she went far out with her father to fish or sought among its waves for shells. What matters is that Guntur had discovered another way to make his journey to the afterlife.

Where would the journey begin?

In the same place it would end. In his shadow theater, in his mind, in time and outside of it—in a place where all these things are the same.

With words.

Guntur took down the story-screen. Except for

Arjuna, the *wayang* would remain in their chests. No shadows would be made to fall on the white cotton.

Eyes shut, Guntur told his dream of Candra and the island. Together with Arjuna, he stepped out over the abyss on a bridge of words. Words wed to his puppet's movements like a song to its music. But Guntur could advance no farther than the sea's edge. When the waves withdrew, he saw nautilus and amphora shells. He saw the rut cut into the stiff sand by the boat's keel. And when the wind lay down, he thought he heard the singing fish; and when it stood up, he thought he smelled cinnamon. But the sea brought him to a standstill. He could neither walk on it nor fly over it—not even on the back of Arjuna, whose protector is the Lord Krishna. Neither could he float upon it: the boat that had crossed rivers was unseaworthy and had to be abandoned, along with the elephant that had carried it.

Guntur was forced to return to the playhouse. Disheartened, he slept while Arjuna rested in a banana tree's hollow, green trunk.

The boat and the elephant—were they real?

They had the reality of dreams, the substance of thought; they were real in the way that words are real, or shadows, or music in the mind is. Guntur imagined and spoke them into being. He pronounced "elephant" and "boat" with the same voice that said also "mountain" and "sea." His mind beheld them as one might from a mountain's summit view suddenly the sea and next to it an elephant and a boat. His words sounded in his mind's retreating darkness; and as the darkness lifted like a black mist, things that had been hidden were uncovered. Their forms, dimensions, and weights could be appreciated by the mind. They had the reality of a story, which substantiates itself by its power to invoke the unseen. Boat and elephant were, both of them, real—alive within the space of Guntur's theater and his mind, both verging on the limitless.

Guntur no longer needed the *wayang* to create; he required only the incantation of a story. He kept the puppet Arjuna but renounced the demigod and its energies. Arjuna, the invisible force, was shut out with the other unseen powers, whose talismans were locked inside the teak chests. Where once gods and warriors, princes and demons had cast their limitless shadows from an aboriginal world into ours, now the phantoms of Guntur's mind thronged the theater. It was no longer sacred—no longer a place consecrated to the forms and ways of the past. By his iconoclasm, Guntur disturbed the order of the world. Whether his end was a punishment for his trespass or only an accident is not known, although *dalangs* who perform *The Woman with Blue Hands* judge him harshly.

Surely Arjuna was more than a puppet!

He was a son of the Lord Indra and the woman Kunti, who bore a son also by Yama, a god of the dead. Arjuna was also an aspect of Guntur's mind, which manifested itself according to the strength of the shadow master's desire. His repudiation of the spectral universe and its agencies may have incensed the gods. This arrogance—many believed—was the cause of Guntur's catastrophe.

That night Guntur traveled to the edge of the Java Sea and built a boat there just as he had seen it in his dream of Candra's island. When he had finished, he and Arjuna dragged the boat into the water and, pushing it beyond the waves, climbed aboard. Guntur rigged a sail cut from the white cotton story-screen, and the boat leaped over the stiff-backed sea toward the horizon. Although they were accompanied by singing fish and the odor of cinnamon, Guntur could not cross the unmoving horizon; the boat shied like a horse from a hurdle. The boat tacked against contrary winds and came at it again and again, but always the boat gave way and could not hold its course. The sky above the horizon was like a window streaked with rain, although there was no rain and Guntur would have felt not the slightest obstruction if he had held out his hand. It was the horizon line itself that kept them from crossing into the far sea—the running fire that burned in the water below it and the vexed air above it.

This was the story Guntur had spoken, sitting crosslegged on the floor of his shadow theater. Those had been his words; and on them he had walked out into the retreating darkness, like a man with a candle moving through an unlit house.

Despondent, Guntur returned to the playhouse and slept.

When the light went out of the sky, he woke and remembered that the sea in his dream had seemed an intricately patterned cloth, dyed indigo. And when he and Arjuna next came to the horizon and confronted the gate to the farther sea, Guntur recited these words:

"The sea resembled an indigo cloth, which a wind's rough handling has creased."

And the air softened, the fire inside the water was quenched, the horizon trembled and let them pass.

And Gunter uttered one word after another:

"Guntur and Arjuna searched among the red, blue, gold, and green pavilions. Their number seemed countless; the sleeping dead inside them, beyond what the mind could comprehend. The two walked in radiant shadow, looking for a young woman wearing a brown sarong. They spent many days inside the pavilions— so immense was each one. For weeks, they wandered among drowsing bodies bathed in a sea air redolent of cinnamon and resonant with a colored music."

Unable to find Candra, they returned to the playhouse. They sat together crosslegged on the mat and said nothing until, finally, Arjuna spoke.

Arjuna spoke?

Arjuna or Guntur—it makes no difference. It may have been a voice in Guntur's mind, different from the rising and falling voice with which he was telling the story of Candra's rescue. Nothing is certain in this shadowland where art and death converge. It may have been his mind only, or whatever preceded the mind at a time before stories were told but were nevertheless being written.

Who was there to write them?

They were written by time in the dust that time lays down.

And Arjuna spoke thus to Guntur:

"She will be the one with the blue hands. You have only to say 'the woman with the blue hands' for us to find her."

Guntur shook his head. "I'm too tired to take up the thread again."

"You have only to say it."

"I cannot!"

Guntur let his head fall, and Arjuna saw how he was spent.

"You must," he said in an iron voice admitting of neither sympathy nor postponement. In his severity, Arjuna was once more a demigod or else that portion of the mind where temptation and surrender are contested with godlike resolve.

After a silence in which he strengthened his will, Guntur spoke:

"Guntur and Arjuna wandered a long time among the brightly colored pavilions, hunting everywhere for Candra. At last, Guntur remembered that Candra's hands were the color of the blue cloth worn by the Lord Krishna; and without hesitation, he walked into a blue pavilion unnoticed among so many. Moving carefully among the sleepers, he intoned: 'The woman with the blue hands.' Immediately, his eyes fell on Candra. For the first time, he saw her without the story-screen's dissolving her into a mist. He marveled at her beauty, rejoicing that it was untouched by the fire. Arjuna lifted her lightly in his arms and carried her to the boat. Together with Guntur, they brought her back to Surakarta."

How could they have brought her back?

In the only way they could have done: in a story. Storytelling is an act of seizure; the storyteller, ruthless in his desire to possess—with words—the world that he can enter in no other way.

Guntur spoke thus:

"When Arjuna lifted Candra from out her dream of life, the bangles on her arms struck—petulantly—one against the other."

12.

Guntur could not wake Candra from the sleep that clung to her as a mist does the water until the sun, rising high into morning, can burn it off. Hers was not now the sleep in which she was drowned inside the blue silk pavilion. It was a sleep such as anyone living might undergo who had been brought by sickness to the brink of death. She was not dead; and so he let her sleep, watching her the while intently, like someone blind who all of a sudden sees.

Arjuna sat in the thickest shadow, in a corner of the room—mute, his head on his arms, not because of weakness or weariness (for he was incapable of either), but because he was without occupation. He had played his part and would not be summoned to another. (Only his puppet would, after audiences had rebelled at Guntur's heretical idea of theater.) Like the sun's mirage seen everywhere for a time after one has looked at the sun, so Arjuna—also luminous—would remain inside the playhouse until he faded gradually from Guntur's mind.

Guntur was entranced by Candra's beauty. Without the story-screen to conceal her, he studied her face avidly. With his hand, he traced the outline of her slumbering form. He was seized by a desire to remove her sarong but was stayed by a countervailing emotion—part fear, part reverence, both incited in him by the contemplation of a mystery and both comprising love. He could have spoken her awake just as he had spoken her from out the Land of the Dead. But he was glad that she slept, for he doubted he could have looked at her so wantonly otherwise. Sleep protected both of them from the consequences of wakefulness.

Guntur was made aware of time's passing only by the alternation of light and darkness on the face and shoulder of the woman. The silence of the theater was such that not even the sedulous wasp could disturb it. Arjuna sat huddled in shadow, himself no more than a heap of shadow.

The morning of the third day, Candra woke. It might have been that she had first to let her body rid itself of death, as a poison is slow to let go its hold on the heart; or maybe she had given up dreaming only with reluctance. Guntur could not guess what those who dwelled in Yama's kingdom might dream, what quality of sweetness or ecstasy. Arjuna might have known; but he was already forgotten, with only his shadow left behind in Guntur's shadow theater where so many times before, it had been cast from a place that was neither life nor death but partook of each.

For whatever reason, Candra woke to find Guntur sitting next to her.

"Who are you?" she asked, disturbed by the covetousness of his gaze.

"The *dalang* who gave you puppets for the clothmaker. Duryodhana and Abhimanyu have been waiting more than ten years for you to wake." He nodded toward the table in the corner of the room where two leather puppets lay, pelted with dust. "You've been asleep."

Candra let her eyes wander the room. She seemed unable to rise from the jute mat. Sitting crosslegged beside her, Guntur made no move to help her.

"I was dreaming —"

In the street, the iron-bound wheels of a cart

rattled over loose stones, and a shrill voice shouted in Persian a warning to the driver.

Candra wetted her dry lips with her tongue.

Guntur rose and poured water into a clay cup. With one hand, he held the woman's head while with the other he helped her to drink.

"What were you dreaming?" he asked.

"I — I don't remember."

"Try to remember!" he exhorted her, so great was his desire to know the nature of death's dreaming.

But she could not; and Guntur saw in his mind a pale light go out at the farthest reach of experience—heard a door softly close on a secret of the afterlife.

She sat up and, tidying her sarong, looked again at Guntur—this time with recognition.

"You sat behind a white cotton cloth and asked me questions," she said. "I told you stories. You gave me puppets which I pretended to buy with the clothmaker's money. I kept the money to buy a piece of blue *batik* to make a dress for my friend's wedding. I got sick and died." She felt her arms and face, looked at the palms of her hands. "I burned on the pyre."

The shadow of his inordinate grief crossed Guntur's face.

"How did I come to be here?"

"I brought you back," he said, forgetting Arjuna.

"Where was I?" she asked, understanding nothing.

"Asleep in a blue silk pavilion, on the Island of the Dead. Don't you remember?"

"I was dead," she said in a way that could be interpreted either as a question or as a declaration.

"Yes—don't you remember?"

"Why did you wake me?" she asked, perplexed.

"I adore you," he answered foolishly.

She wrenched her body free of the fixity of his gaze—the bangles noisy with her anger.

13.

And Guntur prepared to reenter the world. He scrubbed the wooden floor, washed walls and rafters, removing the papery nest that the wasps had defended tenaciously against the rain, which had found its way irresistibly through the ruined thatch. For many years he had neglected himself as well; and when the theater was restored, Guntur cut his hair and beard and put on the clothes he had worn before his mourning and abdication.

After so long without a *dalang*, the people of the village greeted the reopening of the theater with excitement. Those who had once gone to the playhouse were eager to return and watch the great Hindu and Javanese stories enacted on the story-screen. Others, who had never before seen a puppet performance, tried to imagine the shadows of men, women, and demons slipping among them as they sat together in the darkened house, whose original purpose they had not even guessed.

"They say we'll see Rahwana carry Sinta to his kingdom and then Rama slay the monster with a magic arrow."

"How is it possible?"

"It is their shadows we will see."

"But how?"

"Rahwana and the others are attracted by the light of a brass oil lamp, which casts their shadows into the room."

"They are drawn also by the music of the *gamelan* orchestra."

"And the *rebab* player."

"And the old hermit's voice."

"He is a *dalang*. My father says he was one of the greatest in all Java."

"What made him close his theater?"

"Love."

"Grief."

All the while, Candra brooded in the same twilit corner where Arjuna had sat, silent and ignored. She would not look at Guntur—would not speak to him no matter how he tried to draw her out. Because of her silence, he could not possess her, knowing no other way than by a congress of words.

He would have liked to have said to her:

"When you walked into the theater all those many years ago, I fell into an abyss. The same abyss

I crossed later in the story I told to rescue you. I fell under a spell woven by a beauty I could not clearly see and by a grace I imagined from the lightness of your footstep, the rustling of your clothes, and the music of your bangles. From that moment until now, I have loved you. Though love has laid waste to my life, I neither regret it nor renounce it. I do not know what other men may mean by love, but if suffering has any part in it, then that much of it I do know."

He would have liked for her to have said to him:

"I do not remember what it meant to be dead or what dreams I might have had during a sleep where dreams are not broken by waking. Where there is time and space to discover all time and all space, the stories the dreamer tells himself must be as complicated and endless as the universe. Those stories will be greater even than those of the *Ramayana* and the *Mahabharata*, where time and space are also vast. But that luxury is nothing next to my happiness in once more being alive. Although I must spend the rest of my life within these walls, I am grateful to you, Guntur."

"Do you love me?"

She does not answer, but neither does she turn from his searching glance.

"Can you love me?"

He answers for her, "Yes."

He hears her bangles betray the agitation of her heart, and smiles.

"This is the first time we've looked at each other," he says, or maybe it is she who says it.

"Yes," the other one replies.

After this exchange of words as significant for Guntur as if they were the rings and vows of marriage, he feels an ardor, a contagion of affection, and—yes—the stirring of desire. *This* is what a man feels, he thinks. This is the countervailing emotion—the solace for his suffering. Goaded by desire, he reaches to touch Candra—fearing her rebuff; but she does not shrink from his hand. Instead, she takes it—this hand, which will caress her cheek and throat and lips—and kisses it, if not yet out of love, in gratitude. Guntur murmurs to her words made nearly unintelligible by passion. But he retains his mastery over language, which not even his body's uproar can confound.

"What will our life be like?" in his mind he asks her.

And in his mind, she answers him: "You will be a *dalang* again, and I will serve you."

"I will live for my art and for you," he promises.

"And I will live for you and your art."

"And you will forget the outside world?" he asks.

"All I need of it will come through the door to see the *wayang kulit.*"

But Guntur did not intend to take up his shadow puppets again and, with the buffalo-horn rods, make them move—their shadows, across the story-screen. The *wayang* would remain in the teak chest where he had locked them, and the white cotton screen had been changed by him into a sail. Remember?

Yes, I remember. But did Candra never speak to him at all?

No, unless it was to curse him.

Having once been numbered among the dead, Candra could not now leave the shadow theater. The instant she crossed its threshold, she would fall once more into unending sleep. Guntur had annexed for Yama's kingdom his theater: it was the end of what had its beginning in death. Having traveled the interminable way between the two, Guntur had been initiated into the theater's paradoxical nature as both an outpost of death and a sanctuary from it. The knowledge that she was imprisoned within an exception to death's rule added to her bitterness. She also knew that she could end her misery (which is to say her life) by stepping into the street. Tragic knowledge is an unhappy gift of creation. Candra could have returned to the blue pavilion and her dream, but she did not.

Why not?

She wanted life and was willing to settle for the shadow life Guntur offered her.

She hated him.

As surely as Sinta hated her abductor, Rahwana. Sinta could have jumped from the window of the monster's castle. She could have found release by any number of means, but she did not. Is it so difficult to understand how both women might have preferred even the possibility of life to life's opposite? Candra hated Guntur as fiercely as Sinta did Rahwana, but she could not yet bring herself to walk into death's arms no matter how sweetly she might have dreamed in her afterlife.

Guntur went on loving her?

And also his art, for she and it were aspects of himself. In many ways, they were the same thing. They both had to do with words.

The audiences hated his new play without puppets, props, music, without a cotton screen to adumbrate the invisible, or an ancient story they knew by heart and wanted told again.

During the time when he had strained the resources of his art to bring Candra back from the dead, Guntur had refined his storytelling practice until the shadow theater was reduced to a voice only—his, speaking, in the dark, words prompted by his own dark imagining. He had thrilled to step out each time over an abyss with nothing to sustain him but an unwinding sentence engendering—by his skillful invention—another which, in turn, lengthened into its successor. Stories— he now knew—were only a congeries of sentences, and the world—he also knew—was a congeries of stories.

Guntur had not taken very many steps across the abyss when the audience rebelled. It had expected a white screen, *gamelan* orchestra, flat puppets shaped from buffalo leather. It had come to see *The Abduction of*

Sinta or another of the sublime texts that were—*mbatik manah*—drawn upon its heart.

"This is not a shadow-puppet theater," one said.

"That was not a story I have heard before," complained another.

"He is not a *dalang*."

"He is a madman!"

Guntur was mad in as much as he was possessed by the principal themes of his imagination, which his imagination had reconciled: Candra and art. His premiere performance had been *The Woman with Blue Hands*—not that which *dalangs* have performed since Guntur's death but an earlier, unfinished version to which he never returned after that first night.

"I wanted to tell them the story of my own search for the love that had been stolen from me," Guntur said to Candra while she sat silently brooding. "I wanted to tell them the story of my sadness, of my brief happiness, of my long grief, and the journey I took into my own heart. But they wanted to hear only what they already knew. Their hearts are fixed."

She did not answer him; her heart, too, was fixed by what had drawn itself indelibly upon it during ten years in the afterlife.

Guntur bought a piece of white cotton. He filled the oil lamp. He rehearsed with the musicians *The Abduction of Sinta*. And he took from the chest the leather puppets, wondering if it was they who had willed their reinstatement.

Arjuna reappeared.

"They want to see your shadow," Guntur said to him.

"What did you expect?" the Pandava replied.

"They could not believe in your actuality without it."

"Do you?"

Guntur sighed.

Candra lowered her head where she sat, as if acquiescing to the executioner's request—or that of the ax.

Her bangles tolled.

"Why will she not speak to me?" Guntur cried, anguished.

"She does not hear you," said Arjuna. "Or only sometimes, the way you hear someone speaking whose words are interrupted by a fitful wind."

"She sits and stares at nothing!" Guntur complained in a voice at once peevish and afraid.

"She sees herself inside the blue pavilion. She sees the shadow that covered her, or the nothingness that is now *mbatik manah.*"

14.

Candra could not rid herself of the feeling she was dead. But not even with the imprecision of memory, which constructs from the ruins of time a replica of a vanished past, could she invoke her experience of the afterlife. Had any of the possible sensations felt in that remote existence been present—however faintly—to her waking or dreaming mind, she could not have conveyed them to Guntur: there was neither a mortal form nor language that might begin to encompass them. Not that Candra searched her recollections or looked into any of her mind's shut-up rooms for things forgotten or ignored. Their mere intimation caused her to shudder because of the living's natural fear of death or because of the desire once more to give herself up to it.

Was Candra in love with death?

Half in love, as are we all.

What she remembered—what she *saw* when her gaze was fixed on nothing was this: herself asleep inside the blue pavilion, surrounded by a multitude of other sleepers. And at the boundary between this—

But she had told Guntur that she remembered nothing.

After a time, she remembered this much: herself among a multitude of sleepers—sleeping and seeing while she slept the island, the far sea, and the far side of the sun separating that fatal island from the world of living beings. She saw them—there is no way to say how it was she saw except by resorting to commonplaces such as: through a mist, or fog, or a pane of water. That last is the least inept of all possible comparisons for how it was that Candra saw from death's magisterial vantage. She saw what lay around her like a diver viewing the distant sky from underneath the water. She was permitted to remember no more of her life on the island—

Her life?

A kind of life, or half life.

By whom, "permitted"?

By the gods, by the inexorable law of the world, by Candra herself. How can I be expected to answer such a question? For her death was an interlude between a past life and a life to come. According to all the sacred texts, is it not always so?

If Candra had not been silenced by death and by the ill will she bore Guntur, she might have told him this:

"While I was sleeping, I saw you coming from far off with the morning light. Arjuna was with you, standing a little apart or sometimes so close that you and he seemed one and the same. You were hunting the boundary between the two worlds for a way inside. I would not have known you were there except for the noise—the turbulence you made as you crossed over finally into that sea and came up onto that beach in my father's boat. It was a commotion never before heard in that windless, breathless place. Those around me muttered in their sleep, as did I to hear it where only silence was heard—the silence of stone—and a song that something even older than stone might sing. I was not unhappy there, nor was I content. Those words have no meaning there. Does one say he was happy or unhappy to have been asleep? Even if you have dreamed a nightmare, it is not a matter of happiness or unhappiness. And so it is in that other life, which is and is not life.

"I watched with my closed eyes how you searched for me—you and Arjuna. So long a time it took you to find my pavilion! (Though there, there is no time.) I did not want you to find it, but you did and still I thought: he will never find me among all these dead! (I did not wish to be found—didn't want to wake!) Arjuna whispered, reminding you of my blue hands. I tried to hide them but couldn't. Movement is impossible there save for that unrest caused by the agitation of a dream. I saw through my closed eyes where my hands lay folded below my breast on the brown cloth of my sarong. How beautiful! I thought. Never before this did I notice how blue hands are beautiful! I did not regret them, though they would soon betray me. I trembled when at last your eyes fell on them and Arjuna gathered me up, as if I were nothing at all. My bangles shook with my fear and anger."

When Candra did finally open her eyes, she saw Guntur standing over her. She did not know him, but she remembered having been in the room—recalled that she had once looked up, because of a wasp's insistence, and seen the rafters.

She seems ...

What does she seem?

That she is no more than Guntur's dream, his

figment, his creature. Obedient or sullen, she has no life apart from his.

He imagines her in every atom of her being save this: her mind's extinction. I mean: what it was she knew or might have known inside the blue pavilion. Because he has yet to know death, he cannot know her innermost portion of—I cannot call it life. But it is what remains apart from Guntur's life.

Why must she remain silent?

So that Guntur cannot possess her story.

15.

A voice in Candra's mind said this:

"When the old man told me who he was, I remembered how I'd felt ten years before, talking to him through the white cloth. The same I'd felt when, fishing with my father, a shark's blunt shadow brushed against the boat. The *dalang*'s shadow made me think of things hidden and unclean. Like people shut away behind the walls of the leper house. I shook with fear and disgust to see Guntur's shadow against the story-screen. I wanted to run. But I wanted a piece of blue cloth! I should not have come back here where I caught a sickness and died. I begged that I might be burned in an indigo sarong; I did not want to go to Yama's kingdom in plain brown! But they didn't hear me—my aunt or uncle, unless the cloth was too costly for them to buy. So I wore this I have on and the wooden bangles on my wrists.

"I don't like Guntur any better now that I can see him clearly, and I'm as afraid as I was before to be alone with him. Not that he has put his hand on me except once when he held my head to give me water. I would die again to feel his hand on me! His eyes seem to rob me of myself just as before, sitting on the other side of the story-screen, he took my words from me. It is worse than thinking of the lepers in their house, to think of him—the way I knew he wanted me. He wanted to take from me all that I am and leave me empty like the dry husk of a wasp. He wants to now.

"I could walk out into the street and return in an instant to my place inside the pavilion. But something makes me hesitate—what, I don't know, unless it's the wish to see what will happen here in this room. Something tells me to wait. So I sit and look at nothing—see in my mind the place where I slept without waking and dreamed what I cannot remember now that I am awake, though it seems to Guntur that I am only half awake. I must not speak—mustn't say anything to him. That is what *he* waits for: for me to speak. It's the only way he knows to take me. I must keep my words in!

"I think he is losing interest in me. Because I do not speak? He has hung the story-screen across the room and taken the *wayang* up again. Poor dusty puppets shut up in their dark chests! At first he tried to make a play without them. Sitting with the people in the dark, without the oil lamp or music. As though they would think his voice enough—telling a story no one knew! Did you ever hear of such conceit? The gods will punish him; he'll go to Yama's hell and I'll be rid of him, and glad!

"He returned soon enough to the old way—shadow puppets, story-screen, the *rebab* and the *gamelan* musicians. All except Arjuna, who rests unused—his rod stuck in the banana-tree trunk. Why? Now that Guntur performs the old plays, the theater is crowded. People sit outside and listen through the open door. Every night, Guntur makes the puppets move—their shadows on the cotton—makes them dance and love and fight. All but Arjuna.

"Sometimes, I seem to see Arjuna in a corner of the playhouse—not a puppet but a man, the one I watched in my sleep stoop down and pick me up and carry me to the boat. He sits, like me, on the floor and broods—his gaze turned to something far away.

"Guntur sleeps all day, exhausted by his performances, which last all night. I never sleep, though he believes I am like a sleepwalker. I wonder what will happen to me next? Waiting is what keeps me here. Half here, for I am also on the Island of the Dead. Did we know, there, that we were dead? I can't remember.

"Arjuna. Such a handsome man! A soldier. I should like it if he took me in his arms again.

"Guntur is famous. From all over Java, people come to see the *wayang*—those ghosts he moves like no one else. Every waking moment he practices until I forget they are puppets. They say he is the greatest *dalang* that ever was in Java. The puppets do seem alive, while Guntur is becoming invisible. I find myself forgetting he is here, until I see him looking at me as if I were water to drink. I shake, then, the way I did with fever. I must keep my words inside, or else he'll steal them. Then I'd be lost. I'd belong to him and not myself. I would have no self—no longer be Candra. I'd be one with them—a puppet without the will to walk outside and end my shadow life.

"Is that, I wonder, what is to be for me? Or does something else wait to do me harm or bring me happiness?"

In this way Candra spoke, careful always to keep her words inside so that Guntur could not steal them and, with them, her. Through the days and weeks and months, the voice inside her spoke while she sat listlessly looking at nothing. All day Guntur practiced with his leather puppets and performed all night the old stories with them. People came from far and wide to watch—shadows against white cotton—accompanied by the *rebab* and the *gamelan*. And Candra, listless, mute, forlorn, sat on a jute mat, wondering.

Candra spoke further to herself, thus:

"Guntur understands only puppets, and in his hands they are nearly living things. They say his puppets are possessed by the beings they are shaped to represent: princes, warriors, gods, and demons, Pandavas and Kauravas, Rama and Sinta, Rahwana, and the Monkey King. That they come from where they dwell invisibly, to sit in the room with the living. They say you can feel their presence in the dark as I do Arjuna's. It is Guntur's doing—his mastery; and now Guntur is disappearing. Will he become one of them—another shadow behind the story-screen? If he is not already one.

"One day my aunt comes to watch. She knows me at once; I look the same as when she saw me on my funeral pyre. In death, there is no age—no growing older. She wants to hug me, to put her face against my neck and cry. But something in mine will not allow it. What, I wonder, does she see on me?

"'Candra! Why are you here?'

"I say nothing, having gotten used to my silence. But she cannot be left unanswered. Anyone would wish to know—insist on knowing why and how! She had watched me burn!

"'The *dalang* brought me back,' I say as if it were an ordinary fact and not miraculous.

"'Why, Candra? Why did he do it?'

"'He loved me.' I shrug—I nearly laugh. It sounds impossible. Well, it is impossible! Yet he did it, and I am here. Half here, half where I was, with silence droning in my ears.

"She is about to ask me whether I love Guntur, but she sees in my eyes that I do not—sees my loathing.

"She reaches out to take my arm. I watch her hand slowly move toward me—across such a distance it seems to come! Her hand takes such a long time to cross it until, finally, I feel the pressure of her fingers on my wrist.

"'You must come home with me!' she whispers urgently. Why, I wonder, does she whisper? Guntur is outside in the street, speaking to the musicians, who are going home to sleep. 'Your uncle is dead.' She looks at me strangely, her head tilted to one side. She's wondering whether I know already that he is dead.

"I shake my head. 'I didn't know.' Am I sad? He was good to me while we both lived. I think I loved him then. How he'd play his flute by the river to wake me gently up. But I do not feel sad. Suddenly, I am afraid because I do not feel sorrow for him or pity for my aunt, who holds my wrist—or anything at all.

"'My heart's dead,' I hear myself say; but it is only in my mind I say it.

"Then I tell her how it is: that I cannot leave the theater unless it is to die again. I don't tell her how that grim fact makes me almost cheerful, like knowing where the poison is with which to make my escape.

"'My heart's dead,' I repeat—this time aloud, but she doesn't hear me, or won't.

"She lets go my arm. 'You can't come home with me then,' she says resignedly and sighs.

"'No.'

"There is nothing more to say. She would kiss me, but the distance between us is as immense as that between Yama's kingdom and Guntur's shadow theater and equally dangerous to cross. Suddenly aware of it, she hesitates the way you would at the entrance to a sickroom. I don't doubt that her affection for me is strong enough to overcome the fear of sickness. Didn't she wipe away the sweat fever had brought out on me? And didn't she wash my body when the life had gone out of it? In a moment, she'll lean across the gulf to kiss me goodbye. I turn away to spare her that. In her eyes, I'm dead—a ghost, and who is brave enough to kiss a ghost? Could I feel anything deeply, I'd suffer to be so unmoved by the sorrow on her face. She leaves the playhouse without another word.

"The next day a messenger from King Senapati arrives, commanding Guntur to perform *The Abduction of Sinta* at the royal court in Jogjakarta."

16.

And Candra never spoke to Guntur at all?

Only to rebuke him after his return from Jogjakarta. Otherwise, she looked into the distance the way you would a river's reach half hidden in fog. Her puppet did, in the shadow play I saw in Cirebon. The words she spoke to herself just now are mine: I gave them to her. So you see I'm not like Guntur. I never wanted to possess a woman's mind. To take her in that way. That was Guntur's way. He was not a man like us. In *The Woman with Blue Hands* the clerk from the Dutch East India Company took me to see, Candra did not speak until the young man Panji stopped at the playhouse on his way to fight the Portuguese. She looked into a distance like a reach half hidden in fog. Her thoughts were elsewhere. She must have been thinking of something! Her head must have been jangling with words! How else do we think if not with them? I gave her mine so that you could see her live—unlike Guntur, who would have robbed her of them.

She saw Arjuna sitting in the corner. She thought of him.

In this story I am telling you, Candra thought of Arjuna. Stories make their own demands on truth.

Had Guntur lost all interest in her?

He had believed his artistry could woo and win her. You see how little he knew women! And because she wouldn't speak to him, he could not shape her to his own design. She wasn't a piece of cloth waiting to be dyed! There would be no *mbatik manah*: Guntur could not inscribe himself upon her heart. He saw, at last, the dimensions of his folly (it was colossal!) and knew, at last, the rejected lover's humiliation. So he seemed to forget her, the same as he had Arjuna. His art once more absorbed him—his shadow theater. But he did not forget her any more than he had Arjuna, who sat and brooded in a corner of the *dalang's* mind. They were, all of them, waiting for what might happen next.

Candra was almost happy after Guntur had left for Senapati's palace. For three weeks, she would have the playhouse to herself. If it were not for feeling she was at flood—her self (what remained of it) in motion toward that far island, she might have been content to be becalmed a while in an ordinary room. But the island gripped and drew her from afar as the pole star does the compass needle. Is this not death itself? Is there not in death an element of desire, which incites a flux of atoms toward itself, though it ends in their obliteration? Increasingly, she felt entombed within her body—possessed of a leadenness that made the least movement of her body difficult. It was this languor that staved off the inevitable. That and her affinity for the theater's shadows. Though the island had been in garish sunlight, the passage there and back had been as darkly lit as the exit from the womb. Did she remember it? I said before that she did not, except for a sensation of having passed through twilight or a darkness riven by lightning. We are grappling with the unsayable! In any case, she stayed despite her other self—the one, I mean, who wished for the—in Shakespeare's word—quietus: an end.

I don't know if I have conveyed to your mind the suspension in which Candra passed her days in the playhouse. She waited like one on trial for her life. She waited like a crab down in the mud for the water to warm and give it back its crab life. She waited like a withered plant for sun. There is no way to say what quality of waiting Candra endured. And yet she did not suffer greatly. She was anxious—yes—and felt within herself tempests of uncertainty; but anguish requires a degree of sentience she lacked. She could not feel, you see—not entirely as those who are wholly living do. They might have dragged her out into the street and nailed her to a tree; I doubt she would have so much as cried out.

The villagers?

They were suspicious of this woman who appeared from nowhere and never left the playhouse. Some believed her to be a witch, most that the *dalang* kept her as his concubine. How little they knew Guntur! (Though in a way she was what they supposed her to be.) But Candra was under his protection, and he had been sent for by the king, and so she was left alone.

Why did Candra's aunt not tell them who she was?

How does one tell it? How does one say, "She is my niece, who died ten years ago. Don't you remember her? She brewed indigo dye, and her hands were blue?" How would *you* tell it?

What suffering was Candra's was caused by loneliness. You might not think that someone whose estrangement had been absolute could ever again feel loneliness. But she did, and keenly. It must be so for anyone who resides (I won't say lives) in two irreconcilable worlds. But she did reconcile them!

Their wresting into a common space is what Candra's presence in that room signified. Impossibilities are nonetheless possible, transformed by violence sufficient to crack the frame of life.

Candra would have spoken gladly to Arjuna, but he was as impenetrable as stone. His presence may have been of a different order from hers, as stone is other than a woman and cannot mingle its mineral atoms with her evanescent flesh. It was not long, besides, before he faded entirely from the room. Perhaps he had been kept brooding there by Guntur and had now returned to the story time and space of the *Mahabharata*; perhaps he followed the *dalang* to Java's royal court. One day she looked and found him gone.

All motion inside the playhouse nearly ceased. Only the persistent wasp beneath the roof disturbed the illusion of perfect stillness. Candra lay on a jute mat or sat where Arjuna had, straining to the limits of audition to hear the crystal waves ring upon the island's shore and the winds sing among the far pavilions their desolate song. No words paced her mind in recollection; she did not think at all. Neither did she sift the sensations of each moment, though to say "moment" is to reckon Candra's state in time: time had also ceased. She was, I say, in suspension—a leaf on the surface of a brook, moving as the brook moves, part of the brook and not a part of it at all.

You could not say Candra lived or dwelled or was

tenant of that narrow space: she had no right to be there or anyplace else this side of the morning sun. She was like a squatter who came in from inclemency to wait for conditions more auspicious for a journey. A journey lay in Candra's future; I've said as much. A journey, the length of that she took once before. While she waited in the empty theater, the light came and went in tides of shadow. The indefatigable wasp rasped. (Strange that there should always be a wasp!) She did not eat; she took almost no water. She scarcely seemed to breathe! The conduct of her organs might have been observant of quite different laws than those that govern ours. Her heart—remember?—she thought was dead. But I wonder if it was? I think it the only thing in her that wasn't, though it beat according to its own slow measure.

Light swept in through the windows. It mixed with the dust while shadows stalked across the floor, then jumped onto the wall to lose themselves in night's black sea. Candra lay on the mat and did not move, and all but her heart was still. There was not so much sound as even wooden bangles make, falling lightly one against the other.

And then one day, a man came through the door, bringing with him the sounds and odors of the street. A shadow, which had been lengthening across the floor, shrank from the sudden light that sprawled everywhere, like water thrown from a bucket carelessly. The man stopped, but his atoms' movement had already vexed those of the room's slumbering currents. Something of him continued to its far corners, lapping the walls and agitating the slender ladders of dust hanging from the rafters. The afternoon light shone behind him through the open door.

Something of those atoms stirred sympathy in Candra. Her inward gaze turned from the blue pavilion while the sound of wind and waves fell to a murmur and, finally, to no sound at all. She was wholly in that room—Guntur's shadow-puppet theater—for the first time since her abduction. (That is what it was, so why not call it that?) For an instant, she thought the man standing before her was Arjuna; for he seemed of no more substance than a shadow with the strong light behind him. But when the door shut, she saw a young man.

"Who are you?" she asked, amazed.

"Rama. I've come to rescue you from Rahwana's castle."

No, that is not what they said to each other. It was rather this:

"Who are you?" she asked.

"Panji. Can I have some water? I'm thirsty, after being all day on the road."

Candra rose and poured him water from the earthen jar. He thanked her, drank, and asked for more.

"I've walked all the way from Gunung," he said,

giving her back the cup. "I'm on my way to Semarang to fight the Portuguese. What's your name?"

"Candra," she answered, lowering her eyes from his, which had been looking at her insistently. Suddenly abashed, he strode about the playhouse floor as if to measure it with rough strides.

"What kind of place is this?" he asked.

"A shadow-puppet theater."

"Are you here alone—you with your blue hands?"

"The *dalang* went to perform at the court of Senapati. Tomorrow, he returns."

Panji made a mocking noise to conceal his bashfulness. Having so insolently appraised her, he could not now look at her, as if he sensed that she would not be made a conquest but would resist every attempt to sway her from herself. Her indomitableness was only partly in her original nature. Death had given her final dominion over her body or her body's semblance. (What quality of presence the body may have had for her in death is not for us to know. True, Arjuna had gathered her in his arms. But what was Arjuna on the far side of the sun? What, in any case, is Arjuna?) Let it suffice to say that in death Candra had severed every tie that binds together the living, one to another, in fiefdom or in love. She belonged to no one but herself and would always until she chose to share herself with someone else. It was her inviolability that subdued the young man's natural swagger. He was a soldier, after all, and could be counted on to swagger before a pretty girl! When at last he set bravado aside in favor of a becoming youthful vulnerability, she smiled at him.

"Have you never seen a shadow-puppet play?" she asked.

"No."

"Sit there," she said, nodding toward a mat while she hung the cotton screen, shuttered the windows, and lit the oil lamp.

He sat and waited for her to choose two *wayang* from the chest. She chose a girl and a warrior puppet, Gatotkaca, the Flying Knight.

"There should be music, but we have no musicians," she apologized.

He offered to whistle or clap his hands.

"Be still and watch!" she commanded.

She handled the two parchment figures awkwardly, and the story she invented for them was only another version of Sinta's. It did not please her, and she abandoned it before Gatotkaca had landed on the mountaintop where the girl was imprisoned by a demon.

"I'm no *dalang*!" she laughed, extinguishing the lamp and returning the puppets to the chest.

"In my father's town, they perform *wayang topeng*. Do you know what that is?

"*Topeng* means mask," she said.

"Yes, people play the parts, wearing masks."

"There are no puppets?"

"No puppets," he said as he took down the cotton screen and opened the shutters. "The most famous play in *wayang topeng* is called *Smaradahana*."

"*The Fire of Love*," she repeated.

"It's the story of a goddess of love, whose name is Candra Kirana, and a god of love, whom I am named for: Raden Panji Asmarabangun, the crown prince of Jenggala."

He stood in the middle of the room, which seemed in the late afternoon light an ordinary room such as a man and woman might live in together. He opened his arms for Candra, but she did not yet take a step toward him.

"Let's pretend we are them," he said. "Candra and Panji of the *Smaradahana*."

Still, she would not step toward him.

"There ought, of course, to be masks," he explained. "Do you have any masks in those chests?"

"Only puppets."

"Then we will have to make do without masks," he said. "We'll wear our own faces."

Candra wanted the young man's arms around her. You must not think her frivolous. While her heart had not perished in death, it was nevertheless transformed. It was incapable of falseness, insincerity, even insouciance. They had been burnt away on the funeral pyre, and what remained to her was a solemnity regarding all things touching the affections.

If the heart has its darkness, fire illuminated hers.

Having undergone the simplicity of death—having been refined in its fire, Candra's relationship to the living world became simple. Her judgment was unclouded by complication or subtlety. She saw into the heart and knew, instantly, the worth of the person in which it beat. Candra looked at Panji—into his heart—and loved him without misgiving.

Why then did she not run into his arms?

She was afraid. She had been a ghost; she might be one still. Panji's arms might have enfolded thin air. Perhaps he could possess her only as the blade of an oar does water. So long as she hesitated, love was possible. Would you have hurried to put it to the test?

Because she would not go to Panji, he came to her.

She did not vanish in his arms.

"Tell me the story of *Smaradahana*," she said, surprised by a smell of leather like that of the *wayang kulit*.

"I am telling it!" he laughed. "This is how the story ends."

Now it was Panji's turn to hesitate.

"What is it?" asked Candra, sensing his disquiet, though he held her still in the circle of his arms.

"I was suddenly afraid."

When his arms had closed around Candra, he saw—or thought he saw—a darkness fall upon her face. The light seemed for a moment to go out of her eyes. They had reached the moment in their story which foreshadows an inescapable catastrophe. He shook off the feeling and laughed and let his hand travel across the immensity that separates every human being, which makes of each of us a planet chasing one another round the sun.

Panji touched her face, traced with his finger the shape of it, and would have kissed her had his shyness not forestalled him.

Candra kissed him.

That was all there was for them here, but not all there would be elsewhere.

He had to go; the Portuguese were waiting—or say, rather, one Portuguese, a soldier with a musket, waited for Panji. Candra, too, must wait: for Guntur. They were—Candra and Panji, both—helpless against their separate destinies. Yet fate had reserved for them a convergence for which neither of them would have long to wait.

He begged a gift—something of hers to take with him to the war.

She gave him one of her bangles. In return, he gave her a piece of indigo cloth he had bought as a present for his sister.

"The cloth is the color of your hands," he said in a voice expressing wonder that it should be so. He might have taken her hand impulsively in his, even brought it gratefully to his lips; but he did not. What stayed his hand from taking hers was a third presence in the room, created by a part of him and a part of her, which each had ceded to the other. It had the strength to subdue them both. That presence was love, of course, which has in it always a particle of fear.

17.

That Candra and Panji should also be two lovers in the Smaradahana is hardly likely.

Is it likely that Oedipus would marry his mother? And yet for Oedipus, it was inevitable. In Vlissingen once, I saw the body of a man wash up. When it was turned over, I saw how the crabs had eaten him. He had been in the water a day, according to a ship's surgeon who happened to be there. The morning when the man had rowed out to fish, or had been plying his marlin spike on the deck of some merchant ship, or had leaned over the railing of a belvedere, waiting for the time when he might go into breakfast—however that man had begun the day that would be his last, neither he nor anyone who knew him would have believed it probable that he would end a feast for crabs. In Vlissingen! Had he been waiting for them and the crabs for him? Or had he and they merely, by some strange chance, converged? In either case, the drowned man could not have prevented that tragic convergence any more than Oedipus his. Were those conjunctions any less improbable than Candra and Panji's meeting, or that he should have in his soldier's pack the very thing for which she'd longed the week before she died?

Next day when Guntur returned from Jogjakarta, he found Candra, like a town prepared for siege, fortified against him. No longer mute, she was ferocious in her scorn as if the freshet of her love had spawned a bitter tributary of hate. Love or enmity, neither could be trivial for one whose heart had been milled of all impurity by death. Guntur soon regretted that he had ever wished for her to speak.

"You are ungrateful!" he rebuked her.

"I never asked for this!" Her fury nearly felled him.

Guntur had arrived in Surakarta that afternoon, jubilant. His success at court had been remarkable: Senapati had pronounced him Java's greatest *dalang*. The king had urged him to remain in Jogjakarta and establish a school for shadow masters. But because of Candra, Guntur could not accept his offer; and the king wisely did not make it a royal command. On the road home, Guntur had persuaded himself that his new fame would impress the silent woman— might even excite in her love. He would have been satisfied with its counterfeit. He believed that she was incapable of an emotion that was not adulterated by death. He reasoned that it could not be otherwise. Her heart was like a quarried stone. But Guntur did not know that it had been warmed by love as an unearthed stone is by the sun.

He was wearing clothing made of gold-lead *prada* cloth presented to him by Senapati. His success had transformed him: his bearing, even his face, seemed to belong to another man. Entering the playhouse in his finery, he was prepared to court the young woman with the confidence of someone else. The pretense lent him a tyrannical majesty. He expected her to turn instantly from her rapt contemplation of the invisible—to close the distance between past and present in a rush of astonishment. Instead she raged, and his majesty deserted him. Suddenly, he saw himself as ridiculous and turned cruel.

They struggled now against each other. And with them always in that room was the presence Candra and Panji had invoked, like the atmosphere inside van Musschenbroek's Leyden jar.

Still, Guntur did not wish her gone. Perhaps he hoped that she would one day turn kindly toward him, or he may have seen her as evidence of his ultimate mastery over the shadow world—a sacrilege he dared not reveal. And because she was waiting for Panji, Candra would not leave the playhouse. What life she might have imagined for them both is impossible to tell.

Guntur's celebrity grew. He had the playhouse enlarged to accommodate his admirers, who came from all over Java and even from Bali to see him move the *wayang kulit*. During those months, he ascended to a level of mastery that seemed to many supernatural. Some said Guntur was under the patronage of the Lord Krishna himself, who might have been seen sitting crosslegged on the floor beside him, just as he had stood by Arjuna in the Pandavas' war against the Kauravas. But Candra's rancor spoiled the master's triumph.

"Am I so ugly, so old a man that you cannot love me?" he asked.

"Twice, you behaved contrary to nature and to *dharma*," she replied. "The first time was when you allowed yourself to love a woman so much younger than yourself; the second, when you brought me back from the dead."

Later he asked, "Since we must live together, can we not do so as friends?"

"No," she replied, showing such contempt that he wanted to strike her. But he could not know what power she might possess, what capacity for retaliation borrowed from the dark gods of the afterlife.

Still, he would not part from this woman who had made of his longing a kind of pyre on which he burned. He might have eased himself in the house where he had used to go. But he preferred the torment of an unrequited love. It is often so.

What company he kept was with the musicians, with whom he sometimes drank, and with his puppets, whose power of speech did not in the least surprise him. Candra kept to herself in a part of the playhouse used for storage and rehearsal. No one thought anymore about the sullen woman who never left the shadow theater. She made a dress from the blue cloth, then set it aside against the day when Panji would come back for her. That he would return, she was certain; she loved as she hated, beyond the shadow of doubt.

She would close her eyes and think of the bangle she had given him. The thought of it brought her to his arms, which closed about her. To wait did not distress her, nor did she suffer by his absence. Having died, she could no longer measure time—with what speed it passed or even if it passed at all. Time flowed for her like an ocean sweeping round a buoy. She rested, untroubled, in time's backward or forward movement. It was this self-possession that made her appear withdrawn. She was like Dr. Franklin's conducting rod, which takes the temperature of the moment, returning always after a moment's excitation to its inert self.

She did not remember herself as a girl; indeed, she recalled nothing of her life. What memories she had of the afterlife (beyond the slight impressions she had formed of it) were her observations of the mortal world. "Observations" is not apt; but there is no word to convey with what passivity she entertained the distant, living world or by what extrasensory organs she had news of it. For convenience, then, let's say that the mortal world she *felt* inside the blue pavilion was limited to Guntur's theater during the years in which he had attempted, like a repeatedly rebuffed explorer of the Pole, to reach her. She had felt a noise, a vague commotion like a rumor of war at a remote frontier.

After she had finished making the blue *batik* dress, Candra grew still. She stayed in the playhouse— inert—as if waiting for an electric bolt to animate her. Although she would not have said she waited— could not realize that it was so—she was, nonetheless, waiting for Panji.

Guntur became corrupt. Surfeited by the ethereal, he acquired Japanese vases, Chinese scrolls, Persian and Indian miniatures, Russian icons, exotic instruments. It did not matter what he bought with the stipend Senapati gave him so long as he could surround himself with objects whose properties could be discerned by any ordinary man. Guntur had had enough to do with ghosts. The lover's malady that he had nursed with perverse devotion also sickened him, and he sought at night once more for remedies in the marketplace.

While his artistry remained supreme, it no longer had about it intimations of the sublime. His performances became earthbound: where before Gatotkaca seemed himself to fly without Guntur's intervention, his flights now became mechanical—the result of Guntur's cunning manipulation of the rods. Not that the audience noticed any difference in Guntur's performances; only another master of the shadow theater would have been aware of the decline. Another *dalang* might have guessed that the ghosts—the primeval energies peopling the *Ramayana* and *Mahabharata*—no longer came as readily to Guntur's hands. Had the decline continued unchecked, they would not have come at all, and Guntur's theater would have become secular. A Punch and Judy show.

One winter, which has a graver meaning for us Dutch than for those in a tropical land, a soldier came to the theater, looking for Candra. He was not Panji. Guntur was at a wine shop, but one of the musicians took him to her.

She was standing in the middle of the darkening room. The soldier did not have to give her the bangle for her to know the reason he had come. He rushed toward her, or so it seemed to her. Panji's death—the jolt of it—had immersed her once more in time. Like a buoy suddenly unmoored, she was caught in the surging flood of time and swept into the street, which led to Panji. She had barely time to slip the bangle on her wrist and dress herself in indigo.

Did she choose death, or was she caught up in the moment's urgency, or was it the final movement in the tragic convergence?

The story answers one way, life another according to their separate ends, which sometimes are the same.

18.

Guntur is once again undone by grief. He weeps but is not inconsolable, for he knows how Candra can be restored, by what secret ways she can be brought back. He asks two Sikhs, watching him kneel beside her in the street, to carry the body into the theater. Her arm falls when they pick her up, and the bangles on it click mockingly.

They lay the woman on a mat. Guntur is amazed that her body should still be young and feels anew his age and how much closer he has come to death. He mumbles something to the men, giving each a coin; and they leave without a word.

"Ungrateful!" Guntur rebukes the body in its fine blue *batik*, whose hands even now are stained indigo. "I brought you back! Who," he asks it, "will do as much for me?" Knowing that no one will, he imprecates the night that has claimed once more the world within and without the shadow theater. So taken up with blasphemies (incited by wine and treachery), he forgets Candra. Now it is for himself he weeps as he falls to sleep on the floor.

Guntur dreams that it is he who is lying on the mat while around him the ghosts of his puppets gather. They do not mourn him; they merely look as one does at something that arouses curiosity. Among them, Guntur sees his father and the old *dalang*, who gave him his theater and then went to live a while by the sea. Guntur dreams until he hears a faraway roaring, which may be the sea or time.

He wakes in the dark and rummages in a chest for Arjuna, whom he has not held since they two brought Candra back to life. "Will you come again from your shadow world?" Guntur asks it. "Or have I lost the power to conjure the invisible?" The warrior puppet feels strange in his hands.

Guntur lights the oil lamp, sits crosslegged on the floor, and with Arjuna in his hand, he begins to say again the words that once before transported them to the Island of the Dead.

"You mustn't!" a woman admonishes Guntur, taking Arjuna from him. "You mustn't!" she repeats, roughly handling the puppet.

It is Candra's aunt, who has interrupted the words of invocation. Her face is gilded by the flaming lamp. While Guntur dreamed, the Sikhs related in the marketplace how the silent woman in the playhouse had walked into the street and died.

For love, it is rumored.

"Who are you?" asks Guntur.

"Candra's aunt."

"I did not recognize you," he says.

"You destroyed her once already—now let her be!"

Guntur feels the strength of his resolve weaken.

"I can bring her back," he says.

"She chose death."

"Chose?"

"She was not happy here."

"Who says this?"

"The gods would not forgive your arrogance if you were to bring her back a second time."

"They come and go at my pleasure!" Guntur blasphemes.

Silence, such as one might know under the earth, descends on the shadow theater, while the fire of the oil lamp spills its light onto the floor, splashing the walls with gold.

Guntur sits crosslegged on the mat with Arjuna and begins to recite once again the story of *The Woman with Blue Hands*...

In Java during the reign of King Senapati, the most celebrated of all dalangs *was found dead among the ashes of his shadow theater. Whether it was Candra's aunt or Arjuna, the bright one, who tipped the lamp's flaming oil onto the mat is not known.*

ABOUT THE AUTHOR

Norman Lock has written novels and short fiction as well as stage, radio and screen plays. He received the 1979 Aga Kahn Prize given by *The Paris Review*. He is a recipient of a 1999 fellowship from the New Jersey Council on the Arts and a 2009 fellowship from the Pennsylvania Council on the Arts—both for fiction. His novel *The King of Sweden* was recently published by Ravenna Press. Norman lives in Philadelphia with his wife, Helen.